HEART of STONE

STONE BROTHERS BOOK 2

NEW YORK TIMES BESTSELLING AUTHOR
TESS OLIVER
ANNA HART

Heart of Stone

2nd edition

Copyright © 2024 by Tess Oliver and Anna Hart

All rights reserved.

No part of this book may be reproduced in any form or by any electronic or mechanical means, including information storage and retrieval systems, without written permission from the author, except for the use of brief quotations in a book review.

ISBN: 9798884764736

Imprint: Independently published

ONE

AMY

It was a ripping sound that woke me from the strange dream that, among other things, included the fuzzy handlebar mustache of the customer who'd kept ordering whiskey sours and only drank half of each glass. The mustache had fallen off onto the toe of my shoe, and as it crept up my leg, I reached down to pull it off. The ripping sound followed me right into my dream, giving the weird mustache attack sound effects.

My head felt heavy with fatigue as I lifted it from my pillow. Lazy Daze had been extra crowded and the customers were extra needy. Mom had been sitting up in her room drawing question marks all over a piece of paper when I came in. I let her continue. After a long day of work, I was always glad when she didn't want to have one of her bizarre chats. I'd gone into my room, smoked half a joint and fallen into bed.

It was still dark inside the room and outside the faded, threadbare curtains on my window. Another ripping sound. My head was still in that weird groggy zone as I shuffled out of my bedroom and down the shadowy hallway. I followed the thin stream of light coming from the kitchen and briefly wondered what the hell my crazy ass mom was up to this time. Lately, it seemed that the voices in her head were talking way louder than me. I couldn't ever seem to talk any sense into her. She was heading for a cliff, and I had no way to talk her down from it. Every social worker who visited the house had told me I needed to get her into a psychiatric hospital, but I knew that would only make her worse. And I'd be completely alone.

I stepped into the kitchen, but Mom didn't turn around. Strips of masking tape were stuck in large Xs across all the cabinets and drawers. She'd even taped shut the refrigerator and the toaster oven. She'd pulled my sweatshirt on over her robe, an interesting fashion statement even from her, a woman who lately had decided to wear a beach towel as a cape around her shoulders like a little kid pretending to be a superhero.

Mom's thin, shaky fingers gripped another piece of tape, and her arm swung out to free an extra long strip. This particular piece of tape was not going to go easily to its new kitchen cupboard destination. It folded back on itself and then got worse when Mom tried to untangled it. Finally, she gave up, rolled the tape into a ball and threw it on the floor. It bounced and landed next to a collection of other failed attempts.

"Mom," I said quietly. I knew when she was in one of her manic modes she startled easily, and I didn't want to get crowned in the head with a ring of masking tape. She still hadn't heard me. The voices were too loud, drowning out me and any spark of reason or rational thought. "Mom," I said a little louder.

She continued pulling off a strip of tape. She pressed it across the cereal cupboard, making sure to seal it down tight. Our shabby kitchen was going to look even worse after this little episode of lunacy.

I walked up to where she was standing and leaned forward so she could see me. She glanced my direction. I had inherited my mom's green eyes and her smile, according to people who knew us. I'd always been glad to hear it. My mom's smile was her best feature. Of course, my shitty dad, who had been an even worse husband, rarely gave her a reason to smile.

Mom continued with her taping task, basically ignoring me. I put my hand on her arm so she'd focus on my face. Sometimes, it seemed she had to read my lips to hear me over the voices. She blinked at me almost as if she was seeing me for the first time ever. "Amy?"

"Mom, why are you taping shut the kitchen cupboards?"

A tiny grin curled her lip as if she knew a secret that no one else knew. "Because that's how they are trying to get inside the house. They enter right through the cabinets. But I'll make sure they don't get in." She spent a few patient seconds trying to free the edge of the tape and then yanked off a long piece.

I stood there and watched her for a few moments, wondering just when her mind had reached that point of no return. For a long time, she'd just been sad, incredibly sad. The depression had really taken hold a few years before my dad drowned, when he'd grown extra bitter and unbearable. During those horrid years, when his fishing skills and luck seemed to have dried up and he was taking his crappy life out on us, Mom and I would scoot around the house like shadows trying not to be noticed. Looking my dad in the eye would trigger interaction, and interaction always ended badly.

That awkward existence of trying to stay invisible had sent my mom into a state of despair that'd robbed her of her very soul. She'd gone from being the woman who made me homemade granola and helped me with a long division problem at the kitchen table to a lump of gray, lifeless skin and bones. For the longest time, I'd hoped the sadness would go away. Now it had. But it had been replaced by something much scarier.

Mom continued to secure our kitchen against invasion by the alien beings who she'd convinced herself were constantly watching the house. I grabbed my coat off the hook and pulled it on over the t-shirt I'd worn to bed. I opened the front door. The usual smell of the ocean had been replaced by the wet, static-charged smell that preceded a thunderstorm. The trees were bowing their heads in unison as a strong wind pushed the clouds across the bay. The stars and moon had been obliterated, leaving behind a dreary, cold night where the only illumination was coming from a few of the fizzling porch lights in the neighborhood.

My feet were numb with cold by the time I crossed the patch of weeds to Hunter's front porch. The house was dark, but not because the brothers were sleeping. Hunter and Slade never fell into bed before dawn. I told them it was like living next door to vampires.

Colt and Jade had moved into the beach cottage permanently, and on nights like this, when my mom was acting extra nuts, I missed having Jade nearby. We'd become best friends so fast, I couldn't remember a time when I hadn't known her. We were connected by the Stone brothers and by something much deeper, a sort of understanding about just how ugly the world could be and how hard you had to work to not let the bad stuff swallow you up. She had Colt's undying love though. And I had Hunter. But I had slowly come to grips with the harsh reality that Hunter Stone had no love to give. We were together all the time, but just like his motorcycle and his boat, I was only an object that he didn't want to be without.

I sat on the porch deciding to stay outside until our kitchen light went out and Mom went to bed. With a storm rolling in and a black sky above, it should have been extra cold, but the clouds were acting like a tarp, a thick cover that had trapped in some of the day's lingering heat.

A single headlight lit up the street as Hunter's motorcycle rumbled around the corner. His massive shoulders spanned far wider than his handlebars as he turned the bike up the driveway. He hadn't bothered with a helmet tonight. The ride had blown his dark hair into a wild array of black spikes. Even in the nearly lightless night, I could see every plane and angle of his handsome face. I had it memorized. I had the whole fucking man memorized.

I could still remember the day when the notion that I loved Hunter had fallen on me like a ton of bricks. My dad had come home after a particularly bad day of fishing. I'd stupidly spoken back to him when he told me to get the hell off of his couch. His hand came at me so fast, I hadn't even seen it coming. A splash of pain followed that left me dazed for several seconds. Also avoiding the wrath of their old man, Hunter, Slade and Colt had been tossing a football in their front yard when I shot out of the house. I was crying uncontrollably as I raced straight into Hunter's arms. All the brothers were important to me and I'd do anything for them, but it was Hunter who I wanted when things were really bad.

Hunter climbed off the bike and stretched to full height. His enormous size made the motorcycle look like a toy. His long legs carried him toward the house. He hadn't noticed me yet, sitting there, skulking in the darkness.

"Why so early? Couldn't find any sweet necks to bite?"

His face popped up. "Street, shit, why are you crouched out there on the porch?"

The wind snapped through the massive tree in front of the house. It was the only vegetation still clinging to life in their barren front yard. A hurricane of orange leaves fluttered to the ground.

I wrapped my arms around my knees and pulled my legs closer to my chest. "I'm watching the clouds roll in."

"Looks like it's going to be a big storm." The porch steps creaked beneath Hunter's weight. He sat down next to me. His warmth immediately comforted me.

"Remember that time when my cat chased the lizard up that tree?" I asked.

"Then the cat got stuck and you climbed up to free her and you got stuck," he continued.

"And then you came up to get me." I laughed. "It always reminded me of that book they read in school with the old lady swallowing the fly."

"I just remember falling on the sidewalk after the branch snapped. It was a painful but quick way to get down from the tree. I should have predicted that ending though. Crazy shit always followed you around."

I grew quiet for a second and thought about the unsettling scene I'd just left in my house. "My mom was taping up the cupboards so that the aliens don't get inside. I decided to walk outside and wait for them. Figured being kidnapped, studied and eventually dissected by green men would still be better than living with my mom."

"You need to send her to one of those institutions where she can get some help."

A wry laugh spurted from my mouth. "Help? You just used the word *institution*. Does an institution sound the least bit helpful?"

He sighed loudly and a cloud of beer breath followed. "I'm just saying there might come a time when you can't handle her craziness anymore. She's too much, Amy. She's going to hurt herself, or worse, she might hurt you."

Hearing him call me by my name always sent me off balance for a second. He only said it when he was trying to sound fatherly or serious, like now. Otherwise, I was

Street, or Street Corner Girl, a nickname the Stone brothers had come up with when I was twelve and in a desperate attempt to make money, I'd turned my corner lemonade stand into a kissing booth. "She's the only family I've got." I shot to my feet and had every intention of marching back inside. But his giant hand wrapped around my arm, and he pulled me onto his lap.

"That's not true and you know it. I'm your family. Colt and Slade are your family."

My throat tightened as he said it. Growing up, the four of us had been stuck in similar slices of hell. But as bad as my father had been, he was fucking Santa Claus compared to their dad, Hank. Sometimes it seemed impossible that they'd all survived to adulthood. But they had, and while they weren't leading completely respectable lives, and while a lot of the people in town made a point of crossing the street to not have to pass them on a sidewalk, they'd all grown up with the innate sense that cruelty was wrong. An unintentional lesson they'd learned from their awful dad. But their horrid life had scarred all of them, physically and emotionally. Feelings and love were hidden under layers of *stone*. Jade had found a way to chip through Colt's rock hard facade, but Hunter was a much harder piece of granite to break.

Hunter tightened his hold on me, pulling me closer to his warm body. The earlier tension drained out of me like it always did when I was in his arms. They were like a steel barrier to anything bad or dangerous in the world.

I rested my head against his shoulder. "Why is it that even when you've said something that irritates me, I still manage to dissolve into a hot puddle of need when I'm with you."

"I think my little Street Corner Girl needs a raunchy roll in my bed sheets." His hand smoothed along my leg and pushed up the bottom of my t-shirt. The cool air brushed over my panties.

"Is that all you ever think about?" I asked.

"I would be lying if I said no."

I peered up at him. "Kudos for honesty then, but I don't kno—" My breath pulled in as his fingers scooted under the crotch of my panties. I was like melted butter in his arms. Hunter knew I could never say no to him. But, sometimes, I wished to hell I could.

Moisture seeped from my now throbbing pussy.

"Ahh, Street, you're so fucking wet, I might have to take you right here on this damn porch."

I curled against him and kissed his neck. "Too cold and the aliens are watching. Carry me inside."

He pushed his finger inside of me, and I arched my back to take in more of his touch. My soft groan floated off the porch and away on the salty breeze.

"Don't know if I can stop, baby." The gritty darkness in his voice matched the stormy night.

I shivered and wrapped my arms around myself to make my point. "A blanket and a warm room. Please."

He withdrew his fingers, and my breath drifted out with them as if he'd pulled the oxygen from my lungs at the same time. With ease, he stood with me in his arms. I clung to him as he opened the front door.

I kissed his neck as he carried me down the dark hallway. He kicked his door open and stepped inside. He walked around the maze of dirty clothes and shoes and lowered my feet to the ground. I'd always been aware of my slight, thin build, but I always felt extra small standing in a room with Hunter.

His brown eyes were glazed with need as he reached for my coat. He pushed it off my shoulders. "What would I do without you, Street?"

"You'd still be fucking every girl in town." I hopped up on my toes. "But you'd miss me."

"Damn right I would." He lowered his mouth over mine. There were times when we'd forego the kissing. It was too intimate. Kissing came with too much connection. Kissing made it harder for me to accept that he'd never give me his undivided love. It reminded me that he just really had no love to give.

Tonight, his tongue stroked my lips with a tenderness that nearly brought tears to my eyes. He was never going to be completely mine. I was his, but a terrible double standard had always been wedged between us.

I'd spent nearly as much time telling myself this was never going to be anything as I'd spent trying to reconcile our lopsided relationship with my heart.

Hunter lifted his mouth long enough to pull my t-shirt off. I was stripped down to just my panties. He reached down, took hold of my waist and lifted me up onto the bed. I relaxed back as he knelt on the floor between my legs. It was rare for him to take the time to make me come first before climbing on top of me. Not that he ever finished before me. He always made sure not to. He could stay hard as long as I needed. And his skill in between the sheets was one of the reasons saying no to him was so impossible. That, and the reality that I loved him so much it hurt to think about.

His fingers dragged my panties down past my knees and off my ankles. I was naked. Everything about the man was powerful, menacing, intimidating. Having him kneel between my thighs made me so fucking hot, I knew it wouldn't be long. His long black lashes lifted, and he gazed at me over the mound of crisp hair between my legs. We never needed to say much to each other. We knew each other so well, it was almost as if he could feel everything I was feeling as he touched me. And he touched me now with that incredible skill that made him so fucking irresistible.

He lifted up on his knees and leaned his massive body over me to kiss my lips. "There is nothing I hate more than seeing my Street Corner Girl sad. It's not natural. When that face has a frown, it feels like this fucked up universe has turned even more upside down."

"I'm not sad." I reached up and touched his face. I rarely allowed myself small intimate caresses like that. They were just as dangerous as kisses. "I just feel vacant."

A sliver of a smile crept up on his face. "Then allow me to fill that vacancy." He sat back on his knees. His hands slid up along the inside of my thighs. He pressed his fingers against the folds of my pussy and spread me wide open. He leaned his face forward. I curled my fingers into his hair and pulled in a long, shuddering breath as his tongue flicked against my clit. His thumb took over as his tongue moved down and plunged inside of me.

I arched my back and pushed myself harder against his mouth. With strong, callused fingers, he grabbed my legs and dragged my ass closer to the edge of the bed. He dropped my knees over his shoulders and pressed his face against me. His mouth devoured me as his thumb massaged my throbbing clit with just enough pressure to coax me close to the edge of an orgasm.

"Hunter," my voice floated through the dark room, "God yes, don't stop. I'm almost there." I squeezed my thighs around his face as his tongue stroked every deep, intimate part of me. "Yes!" I cried out as my body split apart into a million pieces. His mouth continued with a stream of soft kisses until my breathing slowed.

I stretched back with a luxurious sigh and gazed up at him as he pushed to his feet. He reached to the back of his neck and yanked off his shirt. A finely chiseled sculpture of muscle, ink and the thin scars of his brutal childhood, there was nothing more beautiful than Hunter Stone without a shirt.

I propped up on my elbows. "Do you want me to return the favor?" My words sounded long and lazy as if I was still drunk with it all.

"Nope. As much as I love that mouth of yours, Street, the only place I want to be right now is between your thighs with my cock buried deep inside that hot pussy I just had the good fortune to taste." He grinned as he licked his lips. "Can still taste you. I might not wash my face for awhile."

"You're such a pig." I grabbed a pillow and threw it at him. He deflected it easily with his rock hard forearm.

"Yes, I am and you love me for it." He'd said the words with a laugh, but they pierced my chest like an arrow. A cold, lonely feeling swept over me. Love. How the hell could he tease me about loving him when he knew I was completely crazy about him? It was all so damn lopsided. Hunter hadn't noticed my change in mood, and I decided to mask it with a fake smile.

I sat up and kissed his hard stomach as I unbuttoned

his fly. His massive erection was straining to be free of his jeans. I slid my hands along his waistband. As I pushed his pants down, something soft and silky, and very not Hunter-like, rubbed my palm. I stopped. As I reached for the pink silk in his pocket, he tried to grab the panties first. But my small hand reached under his. I plucked the pink fabric and yanked the underwear free. Someone, the owner, I assumed, had scribbled her phone number on the crotch with a black marker. I scooted back on the bed and dangled the panties from my finger.

I swallowed hard and stared at the underwear.

"Street, those— those belong to some girl."

"Well, that's fucking good to know. At least now I know they don't belong to you."

I flung them across the room. "I guess she didn't have a cocktail napkin handy so she just yanked off her panties to make sure you had her number." I kept a cool exterior, but inside, my heart was splitting. I knew he was sleeping around with a lot of girls, but, for sanity's sake, I always just pushed it out of my head. Otherwise, it was too much to bear. But the panties felt like a slap back into reality.

I scooted toward the end of the bed and reached for my own panties and t-shirt.

"Street, c'mon, you know this kind of shit is going on. Why are you getting so bent out of shape about it?"

Tears threatened but I blinked hard to keep them back. I pulled on my t-shirt.

"You know you're my 'go to' girl. You're the one I always want."

"In between other fucks, you mean?" I sucked in a wobbly breath and reminded myself again not to cry. "Hunter Stone's 'go to' girl. What a grand fucking title I've earned myself." I stood up.

He reached for me but I stepped out of his reach. It took all of my courage to look up at his face. His face was always my breaking point. I could never say no to his face, but tonight, I had to place my own heart ahead of that damn face.

I shook my head. There was a flicker of hurt in his expression. Or at least that was what my aching, tender chest wanted to believe. "I can't do this anymore, Hunter. Sometimes I wonder if I've inherited my mom's lunacy. Why the hell would I put myself through all this?"

"Street— Amy— you know how I am?"

One sob escaped, but I tamped the others down. "No, see you don't get to use the fact that you're an asshole as an excuse for shoving girls' panties in your pocket. You have fun with panty girl and every other girl you want, but I can't do this anymore. I need something to fill that vacancy, just like you said. And it's not just your mouth or your hand or that big fucking cock of yours. I need you. All of you. And if you can't give me that then I need to move on." I grabbed my coat and slipped past him. He didn't stop me, and I knew he wouldn't.

I ran outside. Slade was just walking up to the house.

"Street, where are you heading?"

"The asylum, where I belong," I muttered and marched past him. I sensed that he was still watching me for a few seconds. Then I heard his front door open and shut.

I reached my house and peeked in through the window. Mom was still busy taping shut the cupboards.

I turned around and headed down the street toward the marina. The first raindrops fell before I reached the corner. Lightning broke through the black sky and more rain followed. I picked up my pace. Tears rolled down my face as I ran for the dock. My dad's boat, the *Ranger*, had few comforts and the engine hadn't worked in years, but the small pilot house was a place to hide away from all the madness that filled my life.

TWO

HUNTER

The bowls were all in the sink. I grabbed the cellophane bag from the cereal box and poured the remaining milk directly into it. I squeezed the empty milk carton in my hand, and it collapsed, causing a small eruption of the last drops of milk. I threw the squished container on the table and sat down.

I rolled the sides of the bag down and plunged my spoon inside. I shoveled in a spoonful of cereal and glanced out the kitchen window to the house next door. It looked quiet. No aliens, or spaceships, or crazy lady running around with tin foil on her head or a towel cape pinned to her shoulders.

There was no sign of Amy either. Her car was still there, but she hadn't come over, like she usually did, to see what we were up to. Of course, I was pretty sure she came over less to see what was happening in our house and more to avoid what was happening in hers.

Last night had ended badly, but she'd come around. She always did. She'd known me long enough to know I wouldn't change and that I wasn't worth the effort. I'd fallen into bed still rock hard and was tortured by her scent for the rest of the night.

She'd been right about everything. I was a complete asshole, and she had no chance to meet anyone local. Because of me, every guy was afraid to get near her. For a few weird seconds after she'd walked out on me, I'd told myself I had to lay off. I had to stop threatening and scaring away every guy who got too close to her. Either I had to commit or let her go free. But as I let that idea settle in my head, I knew there was no fucking way I could let her go. I couldn't stand the thought of it. At the same time, I was a fucking coward about commitment. Colt had finally taken the plunge into the abyss, and he seemed extremely happy. But he had always been different than me. I was the oldest. I'd lived the longest in this hell hole when the leather strap wielding spawn of Satan was at the helm. More than once, I'd taken the blame for things my younger brothers had done just because I couldn't stomach listening to them get a beating. I had been the oldest, the strongest, the biggest, and

I needed to protect them. It had left my outer shell impenetrable. It was what'd helped me survive. And no one, not even the one person in the world who I cared about more than anyone, could break through the shield of armor I'd constructed.

Slade came down the hallway and into the kitchen. He looked pointedly at my bag of cereal. "Nice bowl. Guess we could turn the water on and rinse some of these dishes."

I lifted my breakfast. The cereal and milk rolled to the corner of the bag. "Why bother when the cereal companies are providing us with these convenient containers."

Slade looked at the flattened milk carton. "So, you finished the last of the cereal and the milk?"

I held the bag up to him. "You want some?"

"Fuck." He turned to the refrigerator and dug out a slice of cold pizza. He pulled out a chair and sat across from me. "Where the hell were you last night? Still hanging with those low-lifes?"

I laughed and waved my arm around the small, filthy kitchen. "Look around, buddy. We're already at the bottom."

"Speak for yourself. Those guys are just fucking trouble." He pulled a piece of cold melted cheese off the pizza slice and shoved it in his mouth.

"Yeah? Then it would be my trouble and not yours. They like to play poker, and I just happen to like it too. Just worry about your own ass."

He put up his hand. "Fine, whatever." He took another bite and didn't swallow before he asked his next prying question. "Why did Street leave here in such a fit last night?"

I ignored him and shoveled out another scoop of cereal.

"I guess that answers my question. You know, she's going to eventually get tired of you and then she'll tell you to fuck off and then you're going to be crying like a big fucking baby."

I chewed and stared at him across the table.

He bit off a piece of the leathery pizza and stared back. "See. You know I'm right. Those eyes already look weepy."

"You're funny as hell this morning. You must have finally gotten lucky last night."

He swallowed hard to get the chewy pizza down and hopped up to grab a soda. "What the hell do you mean *finally*? It's a rare night, my big brother, when I don't end up with some pussy on the end of my cock." He popped the soda and sat down again. "But from that twisted look on your face, it seems that you were not so lucky last night. Did Street cut you off midstream?"

I pushed up from the chair. "Let's drop the subject." I put the remaining cereal into the trash and headed out.

"Again— that answers my question," Slade called to me. "You're going to be sorry the day she walks out of here for good."

I headed out the door. It wasn't Slade's usual warning that made me walk next door. It was my own conscience, something that rarely surfaced, that told me I needed to see Amy. I couldn't stand the thought of her being mad at me.

I walked around to the back of the house and knocked on Amy's window. There was no answer. She knew it was me and was ignoring the sound. I knocked again. "Street, come on. Let me in. I just want to talk." No answer.

I reached up and pushed on the window frame. It creaked open. I shoved the bottom pane up. With the curtains closed and the sun on the opposite side of the house, the room was still dark. I hadn't broken into her room since we were teenagers, but I still fit through the space, barely. I braced my hands on the ledge and managed to pull my top half inside. A floorboard creaked next to the window. I lifted my head just in time to see Amy's mom, Sarah, and the glass vase she was holding.

"Alien intruder!" she screamed.

The vase came down over my head. The loud cracking sound that followed seemed to come mostly from the vase. My skull vibrated, and the searing pain in the back of my head was followed by a hot stream of blood.

"Fucking hell, you loon." I fell back out of the window and into the bristly shrub. Sarah shut the window and locked it, obviously pleased with herself for thwarting an alien invasion. I had to assume Amy wasn't inside. Unless she was pissed enough to stand by and watch me get crowned with a vase.

I wasn't seeing stars, but I was definitely feeling off balance as I stumbled back out to the front of the house. The steady stream of blood had already soaked my collar. Amy was just walking up the driveway. She looked tired and puffy eyed. She was still dressed in the t-shirt and coat. Her long legs stuck out from under the coat. She wasn't wearing any shoes. She hadn't gone back home after she'd fled from my room. Now I wanted to know where the hell she'd been.

Her face blanched as she noticed the red stain soaking my collar and the blood on my hand. "What happened?"

I stomped toward her. "Where did you spend the night?" My sharp question erased the worry on her face and replaced it with anger.

"Sorry, Street, I didn't meant to use such a harsh tone, but my head is splitting with pain and I, no doubt, will be spending the next few hours in the emergency room with some shaky handed intern sewing up my scalp. And I need to know where the fuck you've been." Sometimes the jealousy I felt when it came to Amy nearly gnarled me up inside. It was another reason I'd always kept myself at a distance. I was afraid of what I might do if I actually allowed myself to have her.

"I was on the boat, and, of course, there were three guys with me and we fucked like a goddamn carnival act, trapezes, trampolines, the whole fucking big top show. You should have seen the sword swallowing act." She pushed past me but then stopped and turned back. "And just to let you know, you don't get to ask me that anymore. I can do whatever the hell I like."

I gazed down at her. The image got a little blurry. My head spun and I swayed on my feet. She reached forward and pushed her hands against my chest to keep me from falling on my face.

"What the hell happened to you?" she asked. The rage had faded.

"I was trying to get in your room, and your mom thought I was an alien intruder. She slammed a vase on the back of my head."

She circled around and gasped as she saw the back

of my head. "Holy hell, we've got to get you to the emergency room."

"Might as well. I mean, it's been a great fucking day so far."

"Let's go inside so I can get something to put pressure on that cut. Then I'll grab my keys." We walked across the connecting yards to my house.

"You'd better watch it when you go back to your house. Your mom is taking crazy to a whole new level. You seriously need to have her put away." I was pissed, and when I was pissed, stupid shit came out of my mouth.

Amy stopped halfway up the porch steps. "Have her put away?"

"That's not what I meant, and you know it. My head is ready to fucking explode. You're twisting my words."

She stepped onto the porch landing and faced me. "I'm not twisting them. That's exactly what you said. But why stop there? Maybe I can just have her put down like some rabid animal." Her words sounded choked as if she might cry. Amy rarely cried or at least she went out of her way not to when she was around me.

"Fuck, Street, now you're sounding just as crazy as her." The stupid shit was flowing like the blood pooling on my collar.

"May I remind you that you are a menacing fucking

giant, and you were breaking into the house. Most people would have grabbed something to hit you with."

The head blow was causing my stomach and this morning's cereal to churn, and I was close to puking. "Your mom has known me since I was born. She called me an alien, Amy. She's lost her last hold on reality. You can't take care of her on your own."

She reached for the door, but Slade opened it first. "What the hell is going on out here?" He looked at me. "Fucking hell, bro, I think your brain is seeping out onto your shirt."

That suggested image was all I needed. I spun around and puked off the side of the porch.

I braced my hands on the railing until the porch stopping moving beneath my feet.

I heard the front door open and shut. Seconds later, Amy was pressing a cloth against the back of my head.

I took hold of it. "I'm good. Slade can drive me to the hospital." I lifted my fuzzy gaze to hers. The pain in her face was more intense than the pain in my head. Amy was the last person I ever wanted to hurt, and yet, I managed to do just that every fucking day of my life and I had no idea how to stop. Stopping meant letting down my guard and letting down my guard was impossible. "Go back to your house and make sure your mom's okay." I'd eased up on my sharp tone, but it didn't erase the sadness in her face.

She spun around, flew off the porch steps and ran home.

"What the hell is going on between you two?" Slade asked. "I mean, I figured one day this whole weird thing between you two would just go haywire but from the look of it—"

"Are you going to keep talking while I bleed to death, or are you going to drive me to the fucking ER?"

THREE

AMY

My tires chirped and I flew off the seat for a second as my car jumped from the asphalt onto the gravel road leading to Colt's house. Jade's car was in the driveway next to Colt's truck. I hadn't taken the time to text her and let her know I was coming. The scene with Hunter, a second traumatic blow in less than a day, had nearly made me sick. I was worried about his head, but at the same time, I was so pissed about his usual string of careless words, that I couldn't bear driving along with him to the hospital.

I got out of the car. The house was quiet. Jade had worked at Lazy Daze until closing and was probably still in bed, which meant that Colt was probably still there too. They were inseparable. Their relationship was one of the reasons I'd really started to hate the one-sided relationship I was having with Hunter. In fact, I was pretty sure I was the only one even calling it a relationship. And now that I thought of that word, it sounded completely stupid in my head. God, I really was as delusional as my mom, but instead of aliens, I imagined myself being an important part of Hunter's life. No green men involved but still just as irrational.

I knocked a couple of times and was just about to send a text to Jade when I heard heavy footsteps plodding across the wood floor. Colt had pulled on his jeans but hadn't bothered to button them. I looked pointedly down at the his wide open fly. "Nice look. What if I had been your grandmother or something?" I pushed past him.

"Then that would be pretty fucking creepy because she's been dead for about thirty years," he called to me. "Jade's still in bed," he continued, but I ignored him.

I pushed open their bedroom door. Jade was just stretching. Her shiny blonde hair was splayed out over the pillow, and her cheeks were extra pink. I heard Colt walk in behind me, but I continued to ignore him. He was a Stone, and at the moment, I didn't want to talk to anyone with that notorious last name.

"Jeez, you even look like a damn princess when you wake up," I complained as I pulled up the blanket and crawled in next to her. "You probably don't even get morning breath." I laid my head on the pillow and faced her. "Never mind. I guess you're not completely immortal."

Jade laughed. "What's wrong? You look upset."

"Yep, shit has been blowing through a very large fan since last night." I turned and looked back at Colt who was hovering over the bed with his brooding green stare and messy black hair. I stared pointedly at him. He knew me well enough to know that I was telling him to bug off but he stayed. "Uh, pretty boy, isn't there something you can do? Like polish up those tattoos or brush out those ridiculous eyelashes?" I asked.

"Normally, two hot girls stretched out in my bed would make my pulse race, but since one of the girls is you, Street, I think I'll just go out and tend to those eyelashes, like you suggested. The tattoos are already so fucking awesome they don't need polish." With that, he turned and headed to the door.

"By the way, Slade is taking Hunter to the hospital this morning."

Colt turned back around. "Why?"

"He tried to crawl into my window, and my mom thought he was an alien. She smacked him on the head with a vase." I heard Jade gasp behind me. "He was a little unsteady and he's going to need stitches, but I'm sure the blow to his head didn't make him any stupider than he already was."

Colt stared at me for a second. "O.K. then, I'll just

head out of here so you two can talk. I'm getting some strong anti-Stone vibes in here."

"Good idea." I lifted my arm and waved him out.

I flipped back over to face Jade, and my real emotions poured out. "I'm done, Jade. I can't be around Hunter anymore. I can't just be there when he needs me in bed. Every time I'm with him, I leave a little piece of my heart, of myself, behind. Pretty soon there just won't be anything left. Nothing is going to break through that stubborn pig-ass barrier of his." A sob rolled from my mouth. Jade pressed her hand against my arm.

I sniffled and swiped away a tear. "He fucks every girl he meets and then glowers at every man who comes within ten feet of me. It's not fair."

"I totally agree, Amy. It's not. Have you let him know that you're done with this arrangement?"

"I have. Last night he caught me at a vulnerable moment." I stopped and took a deep breath. "My mom was taping shut the kitchen cupboards so the aliens wouldn't get inside."

Jade's blue eyes glossed with sympathy. I hated being pitied. I loathed it, in fact. My life had always been hard but being pitied was the one thing that made it worse. Only, for some reason, when it came from Jade, I didn't mind. It made me feel better. She'd lived a nightmarish life too. She knew what hopelessness felt like. She understood. "That would have anyone feeling blue, Amy. What are her doctors saying?"

I shrugged. "They think she needs to go into a hospital. But I can't do that. That would be the end of her." My throat tightened. "I'd be alone."

Jade opened her mouth to speak, but I shook my head without lifting it from the pillow. "I know you're going to tell me that I have all of you. I know I do, and having you as my best friend has been the best thing to happen to me since—" I thought about how to end the sentence. "Shit, since forever, I guess. But my mom is the only family I have left. Most of the time she's nuttier than an ice cream sundae, but occasionally, she still drifts back into reality, you know? The other day, we decided to pig out and we made this crazy ass thing I'd found on the internet. It was a frying pan filled with chocolate chips and marshmallows and we dipped graham crackers in it. We sat and watched this old scary movie. Damn are those black and white movies corny. But we laughed and shoveled marshmallow and chocolate into our mouths and watched the stupid movie. It was only an hour or so later when she started pacing the hall with a flashlight because she was sure she saw a strange, red bug climb up the wall. But for that short span of time, with the corny movie and the marshmallows, I was sitting with my mom again. My family."

Jade reached over and placed her hand on my face.

"You do what you think is right by your mom, Amy. It's no one else's business but yours."

I leaned over and hugged her. "I knew you'd understand. That's why I had to climb in the car and drive over here. Plus, it's always fun to irritate Colt. It's sort of a hobby of mine."

She smiled. "I noticed. And you do a good job of it." We sat up and scooted back against the wall. "So, what really happened with Hunter?"

I pulled my legs out from under the blanket and crossed them at the ankles. "We were messing around, and I found a pair of panties in his pocket with some girl's phone number written on the crotch."

"Yuck."

"Yeah, I know. Anyhow, that was it. I just got dressed." I smiled thinking about how I'd left him. "He'd given me some really hot oral sex first, so I was done anyhow. Poor guy was sporting a big ole woody when I walked out on him."

She laughed. "I guess that's the last time he'll make sure to satisfy you first."

"I might have scarred him for life. He might never go down on a girl again." We broke into wild peals of laughter. I pressed my arm against my stomach to stop it from hurting. "Oh my gosh, I broke Hunter Stone."

Jade pulled in a deep breath. Her face was red from laughing. I put my arm around her shoulder. "I'm so glad I came by. I already feel way better. I sure hope the big moose's head is alright. He was really gushing blood, and he was swaying on his feet. Thought I was going to have to yell *timber*." Another laugh spurted from my lips, but this one fell far short of the laughing fit we'd just recovered from. I leaned my head back against the wall and turned my face toward Jade. "Tell me what to do."

"That all depends on what your final goal is."

"What do you mean?"

"Are you really done with Hunter, or do you want to make him so nuts with missing you, he realizes he can't live without you?"

It was a good and completely logical question, but I had no good or logical answer. Deep in my heart, I'd always seen myself with Hunter, but he'd made it clear that we were never really going to be together. "I don't know, Jade. When I picture myself without him, it's almost as if a part of me will just wilt into nothing and die. But then there's another part of me that says I've already wasted too much time waiting for him to come around. I want what you have with Colt. I want to know that Hunter would be lost without me. I want him to wake up thinking about me and go to sleep thinking about me just like I do about him. I want him to feel that same tug in his chest that I feel in mine every time he looks at me. But I've been fooling myself. Hunter doesn't feel the same about me as I do about him. I'm wasting my time."

"I'm not pretending to know Hunter better than you, but maybe, since I see him from outside of the odd little circle you two have built around you, I see him in a different light. There are times when you're in the room and you're busy talking to someone else, even just Colt or Slade, and Hunter doesn't take his eyes off of you." She rotated on her bottom and faced me. "No other guy will get near you because they know Hunter won't like it. That has to count for something. Yeah, it's a thick-headed, cocksure way of showing love, but it might be the only way he knows how. Let's face it, these guys probably never heard a nice word or sentiment of love the entire time they were growing up. Hunter cares for you. You have to know that."

"Thanks. I know he cares about me in his weird, Stone way, but it's just not enough anymore."

She took hold of both my hands. "Well then, we need to help you find what you're looking for."

FOUR

HUNTER

The dusty yellow lamp hanging over the table was making my head hurt, and the tobacco stained walls of the tiny, dirty kitchen were closing in on me, bringing back some of the earlier nausea. I'd known damn well that chasing a painkiller with a couple of beers was going to produce a major buzz, but I didn't give a fuck. The cards in my hand were a fuzzy blur of red and black, but I could see well enough to know I had a shitty hand. I'd spent my last twenty anyhow. "I'm folding, and I'm out for the night."

Sully lifted his thin lip in a snarl. He couldn't have been more than thirty, but he had leathery skin that always looked coated in grit from the road as if he'd been riding his motorcycle down the highway for hours. The asshole always wanted to bleed everyone dry before they left the poker table, but I'd left enough blood on my shirt and front porch this morning. I didn't have any more to give. And my pockets were empty too.

Fletch, a big doughy guy who could suck down a large supreme pizza in one short sitting, grinned over the top of his cards. "There's always the pink slip to that sweet Harley Davidson you have parked out front."

I placed down my cards and smiled. "Hell, I'd just as soon cut off my right arm and toss it on that pot before putting down that pink slip. I'm out. It's been a fucked up day, and my head is splitting. Hey, do you mind if I crash on your couch tonight? I'm pretty sure this fog in my head is going to get in the way of me finding my way home."

"Sure thing, Stone. Just watch the fleas don't eat you up. I found that couch on the end of a driveway waiting for the garbage man to pick it up. Perfectly good couch, except they must have had a bunch of dogs or something."

I glanced through to the small front room where the faded couch was pushed up against the cracked wall. "I'm so fucking numb from these painkillers, they can bite away. I won't even notice them."

Fletch's cheeks wobbled with a laugh. As far as I knew the guy was really sketchy and ruthless, but it was hard to see him as anything other than jolly because of those fat cheeks. "You might even kill them with all the chemicals you've got in your bloodstream." He sat back and the metal chair creaked under his weight. "And with that, I'm out too. You boys finish this round and go home, eh? Sun's going to be up in an hour, and I need some sleep." The other players grumbled at being kicked out before dawn.

Slade had been right. They really were at the bottom of the human chain, especially Sully, who looked like he'd just as soon kill a person as look at them. I'd fallen in with them strictly because of the bikes. Colt and Slade had never shared my love for motorcycles. Slade loved the ocean, thankfully, the only trait he'd inherited from our dad. And Colt liked to build things. But for me, if I wasn't riding full throttle down a highway, I was leaning under my bike tinkering with it.

Sully and Fletch had the same bike obsession. My two shady companions were sort of an unofficial arm of a local outlaw club, not really fully fledged members but rather spare guys for when the club needed something dirty to go down without the official club patch being involved. I knew they were into some really ugly shit, but in their downtime, they liked to play poker and ride motorcycles. So I hung with them.

I walked out to the couch. It looked even less inviting up close. The cushions were stained and dented as if some giant ass, probably Fletch's, had left a permanent mark in them. But I was in no mood to ride home. With the way I was feeling, I wasn't completely sure I wouldn't just ride my bike straight off the coastal cliff. Amy had left the same dent in my chest as Fletch had put in the couch cushion. But there wasn't anything I could do about it. While the doctor had been busy needle and threading my head, I was busy trying to convince myself that I just had to give her up for good.

I turned my arm and stared down at the tattoo of the Led Zeppelin album cover. Amy had never figured out the connection. She'd never discovered that I'd gotten it to remind me of her, my Street Corner Girl. It was a subtle way to keep her with me wherever I went, so subtle that she had no idea it was about her. She'd always just figured I was a big Zeppelin fan.

Fletch followed me into the room with a beer can in one hand and a joint in the other. He sat on the big easy chair, another dumped-by-the-curbside furniture find. He plopped down on it, as I sat on the couch. My vision was still blurry enough to make the crummy little apartment look less filthy. The second my arms touched the cushions behind me, I started itching.

Fletch laughed. "They already getting to you? You must have great tasting blood."

I looked down at the red mark I'd just left on my arm. "I don't see them, but I think the idea that they are here, staring out at me with their little feelers and long teeth, has made me start itching. Of course, it could be the painkillers."

"Nah, it's the bugs." He gulped back some beer and then burped. "So, you tapped out early tonight. Are you strapped for cash? I told you I can get you in on one of our gigs. Nice pay for little work."

"No thanks. The last thing I want is to be tied to an outlaw club. I've already got enough trouble following me wherever I go. I'm good anyhow."

"You still working for Rincon?"

My face popped up.

"Yeah, I know you're running blow for him. I've got a friend who's part of his circle. The guy likes to flap his jaws."

"Great. Just what I need. Colt's already wanting out of the business, and I think when Slade has enough cash, he'll be getting back to fishing like the old man. I can't do it alone, so I'll have to find something legit to do. Probably about time I do that anyhow. I feel like I'm heading off the deep end with the way my life is going right now."

He sucked on the joint and squinted through the smoke as he handed it across to me. "For the pain," he said through gritted teeth. He blew out the smoke. I took the joint from his fingers. "You never did say how you split your scalp." He grinned. "Let me guess— an angry boyfriend caught you in bed with his chick."

"Yeah, sure. That sounds way better than getting crowned by a lady who thought I was an alien crawling in through her window."

He laughed. "What the fuck?"

I shook my head. "Never mind." I took a long hit. It would either make my head feel better or worse. I was leaning toward better because I couldn't feel much worse.

Fletch leaned forward over his round belly. "I think I see a flea on your arm."

I swiped at it and pushed up from the couch. "Hell, Fletch, why don't you take the thing out to the dumpster and give it the final burial it needs?"

He sat back and shrugged. "I didn't see the damn things until after I dragged the fucking thing up here."

"So, because you had to put out the effort to bring the couch up here, you're just going to let it stay, even though it's infested with fleas?"

"Guess so."

"That's where you and I are different, Fletch. I would have taken that couch right back out." I hated it when my brother was right. I walked over and grabbed my coat off the television stand. The T.V. had been broken long ago in a drunken brawl after a poker game turned ugly, but the stand was still in the corner.

"Thought you were staying the night." Fletch said.

"I'll risk the ride home. Better than being eaten alive by fleas. Later." I walked to the door.

"Remember, if you ever need some serious extra cash, we could use a guy like you."

"Yeah." I walked out. A guy like me, the statement swirled through my foggy head. I was pretty fucking tired of being *a guy like me.*

FIVE
AMY

Slade came up behind me so quietly, I hadn't heard him over the clamor in the bar. I swung around with my tray and nearly slammed into him.

He scooted back. "Damn, Street, watch what you're doing."

It had been three days since the broken vase incident. I hadn't spoken to Hunter and I'd successfully avoided him, not an easy feat considering I lived exactly sixty-five steps from his front door. But tonight, my heart had done a quiet flip flop when he'd walked in the door with Slade. Lazy Daze was their usual beer place, and I knew I'd eventually have to see him. But it still took a good half hour to gather my wits after he slid into their usual booth.

"Why are you sneaking up on me like a cat on a mouse, Slade? What do you need?"

"Jeez, nice way to treat your paying customers."

I laughed. "Paying? With the measly tips you shell out, I might even be able to buy a new bottle of nail polish in a week or two. If I save up." I motioned to the carafe of wine on the counter. "Grab that, would ya? This tray is already full."

He grabbed the wine and walked with me across the room. "I know things are kind of strained between you and the giant, unmovable rock sitting in the booth over there, but he's not me. And I'm not him."

"Your point?" I turned away from him and lowered the tray to the table. I placed the pitcher and glasses in front of the customers. I grabbed the wine from Slade and put it on the table.

Slade followed me. "I'm saying— just because you're mad at him, doesn't mean you have to be mad at me."

I turned to him and pinched his cheek extra hard. He winced. "How can I ever be mad at you? You're like a big, smelly stray dog."

"Thanks. And smelly? I think not." He kept pace with me as I hurried back to get more drinks.

"You're still following me," I said.

We got to the bar counter. I turned to face him. As hard as I'd tried to not let my attention fall on the booth where Hunter was sitting, I glimpsed him over Slade's shoulder. He looked handsome and heartbreaking and angry, like always. The only difference tonight was that I hadn't spoken to him at all, and he didn't have his usual bevy of cock groping, Stone brother groupies hanging around him.

Slade almost always had that wry, amused look on his face that actually made him especially handsome. But an unusual serious expression met me this time. "He's hurting, you know? He misses you."

"Really? He told you that?"

"Not in those exact words—"

I turned back around and waved him off, but he took hold of my hand. "Street, you know how he is. Anyhow, look at him. He doesn't even have any chicks around him tonight."

"That's because he's wearing that big, angry Hunter scowl, and everyone, even his horny regulars, are afraid to get near him. Slade, I've got a lot to do. Jack is still out with a bad back. And now that Jade is working on her real estate license and interning with that realtor, she's only working two nights a week. I've still got orders to fill and I'm closing up alone. So go over there and sit with the big grump. I don't have time to worry about him." I picked up a glass and looked at Slade. Just like Hunter and Colt, it felt as if I'd known Slade forever. We'd all survived bad childhoods together. It made the bond between all of us something that was everlasting and impossible to break. Even now, with wanting to distance myself from Hunter for sanity's sake, I still knew that he was a huge part of my life and of who I was as a person. And he always would be.

I pressed my hand against Slade's cheek. He seemed genuinely upset about this rift between Hunter and me, and it only made him that much dearer to me. I kissed his face. "I just need to get out from under this, Slade. I need to stretch and find out who I am, without the massive shadow of Hunter Stone looming over me."

He nodded. "Yeah, all right. Just don't stretch too far O.K., Street?" He got up on his tiptoes and reached behind the counter for a bowl of pretzels. "I figure if I keep the beast fed, he won't take his grumpiness out on me so much."

Barbara, the new server we'd hired to fill in for Jade, had told me she needed to leave early to pick her husband up from work. She waved to me as she walked out with her purse and coat. She'd been waiting on Hunter and Slade.

It was still a half hour until closing, but I was down to just three tables. As the crowd thinned, it grew harder to avoid their table. When Slade slid out and pulled some money from his pocket for a tip, I nearly crumpled in relief. They walked out together. I conveniently walked into the office as they strode through the bar.

It hadn't been easy, but I'd managed to avoid talking

to Hunter all night. I had no idea how long this silence between us would last. It felt incredibly strained and awkward, but at the moment, I was sure I couldn't talk to him without breaking into sobs. And the last thing I wanted to do was show him how hard this was on me.

By the time the last customers had finished their beers, the dishwasher and other server had clocked out for the night. I was left alone to close up. If Jade had been there, she would have stayed to help, even if she wasn't on the clock. But I couldn't expect it from the others. Jack had thrown his back out. His health seemed to be deteriorating with each passing month. He was close to seventy, and retirement was definitely pulling at his heels. He'd talked to me about taking over as manager, but I wasn't sure. Lazy Daze had kept me from living in complete poverty, but I'd never really seen it as my future or career.

I flipped over the open sign and pulled down the shade on the front door. Deciding some music would help the cleanup go faster, I programmed my favorite tunes into the jukebox. Eddie Vedder crooned into the empty room, a space that always looked much bigger after the customers had left for the night. I swept up any tips from Barbara's tables and stuck them in an envelope with her name on it.

I walked into the office to lock up the cashier box for the night. A light tapping sound startled me. Someone was knocking on the glass door. I walked out to the bar. "We're closed," I called.

Jack kept a gun under the bar counter for emergencies. I had no idea if it was loaded because that kind of emergency had never come up. I also figured I was more the crack someone over the head with a bottle type than the pistol wielding type.

I couldn't see past the shade on the front door. Another knock. I grabbed a full whiskey bottle and walked closer to the door. "We're closed."

"Street, it's me." His voice was deeper and sadder than usual.

The usual heart flutters tickled my chest. I took a deep breath and unlocked the door.

SIX

HUNTER

I'd gotten into Slade's car, but as the front light went out and the parking lot went dark, I knew there was no damn way I was leaving Amy by herself. Even knowing I was the last person she wanted to see, I got out of the car and stomped toward the bar. Slade warned me that my pissed off mood was only going to make her madder, but I couldn't cool myself down. She'd been acting like a damn kid, and I was done with it.

Amy opened the door. Her bottom lip turned down in a pouty frown, a face I knew too well and a face that I missed even now as she wore it in front of me. It had only been a few days, but it already felt as if she'd been ignoring me forever. I was done with this silly dance.

"I've fucking told Jack that he can't let you close up alone."

She stared up at me, silent at first but then she twisted that pouty bottom lip, a sure sign that she was pissed. "You talked to my boss? You fucking talked to my boss? What right did you have to do that?"

"I'm just looking out for you because you don't seem to understand that being in here alone at night, especially in this shitty ass neighborhood, isn't safe. Anyone could show up here—"

"Yeah, I see that." She walked to the first table and started piling the chairs on top. "But as you can see, I'm fine. I can use the broom to beat back any attackers. So get out and stop intruding on my life."

I pushed the chairs off. They clattered to the floor. She stared at them for a long second. Her angry, twisted bottom lip quivered slightly. She rarely ever cried in front of me, and I was always thankful for that. Seeing her cry made me soft as fucking pudding, and I didn't need that. "Shit, Street, it was a pair of fucking panties. I tossed them. I never even called the girl."

"Well, you're like a damn saint then. I thought I saw a halo floating over that big head of yours." She moved to slide past me, but I took hold of her arm. She froze in my grasp but kept her face turned away.

"Look at me, dammit." She reluctantly turned her face toward me. Amy could be standing in a sea of beautiful women and hers would be the only face I saw. It was something I would have told her if I hadn't been such a fool. But I was a fool. "You know how it is with me, Amy. Nothing's changed. Why are you acting like this?"

The lip quiver dissolved into a sob and tears filled her eyes. I was just about to pull her into my arms, but as quickly as she'd broken down into tears, a rush of anger surged through her. She pulled her arm from my grasp and began pounding my chest with her fists. And I let her. I stood there and let her swing at me with every ounce of rage she could muster.

"Everything's changed. I've changed." She hit me again. "I'm tired of waiting for a human being to peel out of this steel suit of armor," she sobbed as she pounded me again.

I grabbed her wrists and stared at her. I knew everything about her, and she knew everything about me. I'd been there through it all with her— her crappy childhood, her dad's drowning, her mom's sharp turn toward insanity, and she'd been there for me too. More than once, she'd spent the night with me in the shed out behind her house, hiding me from my dad's wrath and leather belt. She always knew everything I was feeling, but she had never understood just how important she was to me. "No matter what else I do, Street, you know at the end of the day, it's you. You have to know that. I'm sorry if I can't promise any more. I just don't have it to give."

"It's not enough." She turned away from me. "You're turning me inside out, Hunter."

She stood facing the back wall of the bar for a few seconds. Her thin shoulders lifted and fell with shuddering breaths. Then she swung around and pressed herself against me. I slammed my mouth down over hers. It was always raw and easy and natural with Amy. No pretense or fake shit or worrying about pleasing the other person. The connection was solid and real.

I lifted her up and she wrapped her legs around me as my mouth devoured hers. She'd left me wanting her like a fucking madman that night, and I hadn't realized until right now how badly I needed to finish what we'd started. "Fuck, baby, when you walked out on me the other night, I thought I would go nuts." I sat her on the table. She leaned back on her hands as I shoved her skirt up to her waist. Her perfect handful-sized tits pressed against her blouse. I made an honest attempt at unbuttoning it, but impatience and the insane throbbing in my cock made me grab hold of the two sides of her blouse. I ripped it open and the buttons went flying. Other girls would have been pissed, but she groaned sweetly at having her shirt torn open. The only time I didn't use a condom was with Amy. When I was with her, I wanted nothing between us. It had always been that way when I was with her. She wasn't just a girl I met and fucked and walked away from. She was Amy, a person who had been part of me for so long, I couldn't remember a time without her.

Only a few lights were left on in the place. They glowed down on her making her look almost unearthly. To me, there was no one more beautiful, more funny, more goddamn irritating than Amy, and if she ever walked out of my life, I would be ripped wide open.

The round swell of her tits pushed up over the lacy pink bra. Her eyes drifted shut and her head lolled back as I yanked off her panties. "Why can't I say no to you, Hunter? How did you take hold of me like this. I can't shake the thought of you . . . ever." Her voice came out on a soft mewl as I pushed her thighs wide open.

"There's only one place in this world for me, baby, and that's right here between your legs." I opened my fly and pushed my pants down just enough to free my straining cock. She cried out as I pushed my cock inside of her. She was hot and slick with cream.

A tight, involuntary groan rolled up from my chest. "The only fucking place in the world for me," I grunted.

Her eyes opened slightly, and she gazed at me from beneath long, dark lashes as I thrust my cock into her. A mischievous smile curled her lips. She wrapped her long legs around me to pull me closer. "More," she whispered, "I need more of you." Her head dropped back and the table wobbled beneath her. "I want you to split me in two, Hunter." She reached forward and grabbed my face. "Make me scream, damn you."

Still buried inside of her, I grabbed her arms and put them around my neck. My fingers dug into her perfect round ass as I lifted her off the table. She squirmed in my arms, her small, lithe body moving against me as her pussy frantically grasped my cock, not wanting to let it go, wanting more of me.

Crazed and nearly drunk with need, I stomped toward the office and kicked open the door. It cracked off the opposite wall as I carried her inside.

The only light came from a small lamp on the desk and the computer monitor. I didn't need more. I had Amy's body memorized like a poem, I knew every line, every rhythm, every word. And I knew when she wanted it wild and unchecked. The feverish look in her face assured me that was what she wanted now.

It took all my will, but I lifted her off of me. She groaned in disapproval as her feet touched the ground. "I need you naked, Street. I need you completely fucking naked right now." I pushed the ripped shirt off of her shoulders. Her smooth cheeks were blushed pink as she reached back and unclasped her bra. She let it slide to the floor and then reached for my shirt.

"Nope, just you. Naked. Completely mine." I reached forward and pushed her skirt to the ground.

She stepped out of it and kicked off her shoes. She jumped into my arms and lifted her mouth to mine. My tongue dragged across her bottom lip, that lip that changed with every mood, that lip that I just needed to think about for my cock to grow hard. She was so small and thin in my arms, there were times when I had to hold back, afraid I might crush her. I needed that restraint right now.

I lifted my mouth from hers and stared down at her face. "This is where you belong, baby. Right here in my arms, silky hot and willing. You're the sweetest damn fuck in the world, my Street Corner Girl. You are mine. Do you fucking hear me?" I kissed her hard, sure that I was leaving her lips swollen and bruised but unable to stop myself. I took a breath. "Say it, baby. Tell me you're mine."

"Hunter"—her warm breath brushed my mouth—"I've always been yours." The tremble in her voice made me pause but then she reached down and took hold of my cock. All rational thought left my body.

Her small hand stroked me long and tenderly at first, then with an urgency that made me nearly spill my seed right there in her grasp.

I took hold of her wrist. "I need to be inside of you right now. I want you screaming out my fucking name." I lifted her onto her toes for another kiss.

"So what the hell are you waiting for?" she muttered

against my mouth. "I'm yours." Her last words took me past the edge of control. I took hold of her hand and pulled her along to the desk. I spun her around so her back was to me. It was hard to hold back my strength when I was feeling like this, nearly out of my mind with wanting her. I reached forward and grabbed her wrists and braced her hands on the desk. I grabbed her hips and positioned her so that her smooth, round ass jutted out toward me. I shoved my foot between her feet and urged her legs apart.

I leaned back to look at her bent down over the desk, her pussy and ass begging to be fucked. "God, baby, just looking at you like this is going to make me come right here on this office floor."

"Don't you fucking dare." The despair in her tone made my chest and cock ache.

I walked up behind her and reached around, pressing one hand between her legs. My fingers curled through the moisture pooling in her pussy. I stroked her clit. She responded with a soft moan that made my cock strain to be inside of her. Using the hand between her legs, I lifted her ass higher, putting her pussy at just the right position. I couldn't hold back any longer. "Hang on, baby."

She gasped with anticipation, a sound which turned to a cry of pleasure as I jammed my rigid cock inside of her. Instead of moving with me, she moved her ass against me, bracing herself hard against the desk to receive the full impact of my thrusts. It was one of the things that made me nuts for her, no matter how hard I gave, she always wanted more. As if she couldn't get enough of me.

She closed her thighs around my hand, wanting more pressure on her clit. I had to take my mind off my cock and keep it focused on her or I would be done before she came. With my free hand, I reached down between our bodies and pushed my finger into the tight hole of her ass. A low, appreciative mewl rolled from her mouth.

I rocked against her, and she took me in deeper with each thrust. Her body trembled beneath me, and she moved feverishly against my assault. "Yes, Hunter, fuck yes!" She clenched her thighs around my hand as her pussy climaxed around my cock milking me even closer to the edge of no return.

She softened in my grasp and whimpered as I continued to push against her. Her arms were no longer able to hold her up.

I pulled my hands free from her pussy and ass and, reluctantly, pulled my cock free as well. Weak, tiny sounds of exhaustion came from her lips as I wrapped my arms around her waist and hauled her back against my chest. "I've got you, baby. I need you in my arms." It was always like that when we were together. When I held her it felt as if I was holding her heart and soul in my arms. There was no existence past the girl in my arms and that was what had me so fucking scared. I wanted her without question, but the idea of ever losing her was too much to think about. Everyone in fucking town was scared shitless of me, yet I was a big fucking coward when it came to Amy.

She spun around in my arms and crumpled against me. "I'm defenseless when I'm in your grasp, Hunter." She peered up at me with glossy eyes. "I should hate that. I should hate being so vulnerable, and yet, all I want to do is melt into your arms."

I lowered my face and kissed her gently. My cock was so tight, so erect, I could hardly walk, but I swept her into my arms and carried her to the couch, exercising the last bit of control I had left. I lowered her down and braced my hands on the couch so as not to crush her beneath me. "Give me your pussy again, baby. Take me all the way this time."

She reached back behind the arm of the couch and grabbed hold as she lifted her legs up and around my waist. I pushed inside of her, and seconds after my cock was sheathed in the warmth of her moist pussy, I came in a long pulsing wave of ecstasy. It took awhile for our ragged breathing to ease.

I pulled her around next to me and held her tightly against me on the small couch. She always felt so small, so frail in my arms that sometimes I was convinced that I'd just imagined her, that I'd just conjured up this wild, funny, beautiful girl in my fantasy. But she was all too real, and the potential for heartbreak between us was so fucking daunting it seemed the only way for me to survive was to freeze my heart against her. It was what I'd been doing for years, and it had worked . . . so far. No commitment from a man who had a dirty, fucked up past and who had done little to turn things around. I didn't have a damn thing to offer her. She deserved so much more.

She was quiet as she kept her face pressed against my chest.

"Hey, you all right?" I squeezed her. "I'll help you clean up out there."

She nodded but hadn't lifted her face to look at me. "Baby? Everything all right?"

"Yeah, I'm fine," she said as she lifted her face from me. I knew from her tone that she wasn't fine.

"Street?"

"I'm good. Let me get dressed. Then I'll take you up on the offer of helping me close up."

SEVEN

AMY

We'd done a shabby job closing up, and I wanted to kick myself for it. I was sure I'd get a good scolding from Jack in the morning. And he'd been good to me, so I hated letting him down, especially when he wasn't feeling great. But I hadn't been able to work up the energy or enthusiasm I needed to clean the place up right. Hunter had helped, but something told me I would have done a better job without his large, hard to ignore presence. I was definitely sure I would have done a better job if I hadn't caved almost the second the man walked into the bar. When it came to Hunter Stone, I had about as much willpower as a kid in an everything-is-free candy shop.

We climbed into the car. My silence and dark mood made it obvious that I hadn't come out of the south end of our passion scene feeling any better about our relationship than I had going into it. Going into it. Hell, *going in* didn't cover it. I'd nearly jumped the man. Now the bitter ache of regret tugged at every muscle in my body. I could still feel the delicious tenderness in my pussy and it made me that much sadder. It was there to remind me that I was just a fuck to him. There wasn't ever going to be more than that between us. Like he'd told me many times, that was all he had to give.

I turned up the radio to avoid conversation, but by the time I pulled out onto the street to head home, he'd turned it back down. He stared straight ahead. "Talk to me, Street." Right as he said it, his phone buzzed. He pulled it out and checked it, then pushed it back into his pocket. "What's wrong?" he continued.

"That." I waved my hand toward his pocket. "That's all of it right there in a fucking nutshell."

"I'm not following." I could hear the irritation rise in his voice.

"Which girl was that? Or has it gotten to the point where you can't even match faces to names?"

"What the hell does it matter? There's *them* and there's *you*. You're the only *you*. Everyone else is just filler."

"Filler? You mean insulation. Seal up your heart. That way nothing real ever has to happen between us."

He looked over at me. "Nothing real? What the fuck was that back there? Felt pretty goddamn real to me."

I squeezed the steering wheel, but what I really wanted to do was pound him like I had earlier. "You're such an ass. You know exactly what I mean."

"Nothing's changed between us. Why can't it just stay like this?"

"Nope. I'm done with it. Time to grow up, and I guess that means the two of us growing apart." Even as I said it, I felt a cold tremor of heartache rush through me. Just being without him for three days had produced such an urge to be touched by him, I'd ignored all reason tonight. I had to steel myself against him or lose myself completely. "I've figured this all out. Us, I mean."

"Yeah, what have you figured?"

"When we're together, you know, messing around, everything works. When I'm with you, naked and wanting everything you can give— and you do give it well, asshole or not, you know how to please— I'm willing to be completely yours in those erotic moments. You own me when you're between my thighs. But when it's over, I want control back. I want to be independent to do what I think is right and not be watched over. Your possessiveness needs to end when I'm out of your bed. But it doesn't. You have the freedom to do whatever you like but I don't. And I'm tired of it. I have no fucking clue why it took me so long to realize it, but I know it's not working for me anymore."

Hunter faced forward and slumped down in the seat. He had to bend his long, thick legs to make room for them in my small car. I glanced over at him. He closed his eyes, but I knew he wasn't sleepy.

My throat felt as if someone's hand was wrapped around it. "You just need to let go of the damn leash, Hunter. You're free to see whoever you like, and I want that too. No more scaring guys off."

He didn't open his eyes, but his Adam's apple moved up and down along his throat as he swallowed. Deep down, I hoped he was swallowing back regret, swallowing back whatever it was that was keeping him from ever letting himself love me. I had always been confident that he would eventually come around, but tonight, as I was cradled in his arms, feeling every bit his and yet knowing that he wasn't mine, I realized that I'd been kidding myself all along.

We were silent the rest of the ride home. I pulled into my driveway. He climbed out, walked across to his house and never looked back. I had no more of myself to give to him. I was going to grow that same hard outer shell he was so damn famous for and keep my feelings about him locked up for good.

He waited on his porch, and I knew he was waiting for me to get safely inside. It was those small, protective gestures that kept me hoping that he'd eventually come around. But now I realized they'd been just that, small, protective gestures, residual habits of our terrible childhoods when we'd all learned to look out for each other, and nothing more.

The house was quiet, but Mom had left the kitchen light on. Fortunately, my mom's lack of interest in housekeeping had left our kitchen cupboards too greasy for the masking tape to adhere to. Most of it was falling off in long, dust covered strips, making the small, dingy room look slightly ridiculous.

A funny aroma greeted me as I stepped around the corner. An even more unusual sight met me in the kitchen, and it had nothing to do with the masking tape decor. A mixing bowl, cookie trays and a plate of what appeared to be homemade cookies sat on the kitchen counter. I hadn't been able to place the aroma, but I hadn't expected cookies. Of course, it had been so long since I'd seen a plate of homemade cookies in our kitchen, I might have forgotten what they smelled like. They appeared to be sugar cookies. My mom must have had a good, clear-headed night and momentarily lapsed back into reality.

It had been a long night of work, and the after-hours *activity* had left me exhausted and hungry. It was almost comical to think how excited I was to be standing in front of a plate of homemade cookies. A brief, nostalgic memory of standing at the kitchen counter rolling out sugar cookies for Christmas passed through my weary head. I smiled thinking about my mom's face being covered with flour and my fingers sticky with icing. I always made sure to sneak some out to the brothers. I was never allowed to invite them inside. My dad had told me having them in the house was like locking wild animals in a tiny box. He'd never had any compassion for anyone, and he had been only one step behind Hank Stone on the asshole chain. My mom had been one of the people to look the other way when it came to her neighbors, the Stones. She knew their father was a monster, but we were dealing with our own version of monster right in our own home.

I went to the refrigerator and pulled out the milk. My stomach growled as I poured myself a glass. I picked up a cookie off the plate and dipped it in the milk. The cookie was a little too solid to absorb the milk, but I wasn't going to complain. My mom was out of practice, after all. In fact, our oven was out of practice too. I heard Mom's footsteps coming down the hall as I put the cookie in my mouth and bit. A horrid, bitter taste filled my mouth.

"Amy, no! Don't eat those!"

I spit the cookie bite out all over the counter and drank some milk fast to wash away the awful taste. I stared at my mom over the rim of the glass as I swallowed the soothing liquid. I lowered the glass and wiped my mouth with the back of my hand. "Mom, what did I just eat?"

She looked even more distressed than usual as she stared down at the milky crumbs. "Did you swallow any?" she asked.

"I don't know. Maybe. It was awful, so I spit it out pretty fast."

Mom had put together one of her bizarre bedtime outfits of running shorts pulled over sweatpants. She leaned down beneath the kitchen sink and pulled out a box of snail poison. "The cookies are for intruders. If they get in and see the cookies, they'll eat them and die."

"You put snail and slug poison in the cookies?"

"Yes," she said it in a way that sounded like making poison cookies was something everyone did.

I blinked at her for a second trying to decide what to say. I had nothing. It had been such an emotional night that this latest episode of Betty Crocker mania was the last thing I needed.

I shuffled down our short, dark hallway and went to my room. I pulled off my clothes and climbed into bed. From my window, I could see the side of Hunter's house. A light flickered in his room, which meant he was watching television. Just thinking about him less than a hundred steps away made me ache for him, but I had to get past this.

I turned away from the window and pulled the blanket up around me. Hunter's masculine scent was still fresh on my skin. My chest felt tight as I closed my eyes and tried my hardest to push away any thoughts. Eventually, the heavy lure of a deep sleep took over.

EIGHT

HUNTER

A slate gray sky and the sea spitting choppy waves at us made for a rough, gloomy crossing. Seagulls hovered like kites on strings over the *Durango*, a fishing trawler that rarely had any fish onboard. The gulls would be sorely disappointed with the catch in our cargo hold, twenty thousand dollars of good quality blow, a treat for a coke addict but definitely not for a hungry seagull.

Rincon had sent the orders and coordinates for the drop just an hour after I'd fallen asleep. Now the heaviness in my head matched my black mood perfectly. I'd been tired as hell when my head hit the pillow, but all the confusion and crossed signals I was getting from Amy made my head spin too much to let me sleep. One minute she was begging me to bend her over a desk and fuck her, and the next she was pissed and ready to push me away for good. I knew damn well it had always been about commitment, but it wasn't like we'd suddenly woken up in a new world or that I'd suddenly grown a fucking soul. She knew I cared about her, but she also knew she wasn't going to squeeze much more than that out of me. I was fucking cardboard when it came to emotion. Although, there were times when being with her took me to the brink, to a place where I was more human than stone. Like in the office, when our physical need for each other had dissolved into a wild, hot fuck that, just thinking about it, still gave me a hard on. Having her naked in my arms and completely mine for the taking had stirred that splintered, confusing sense of feeling that she had to be with me forever, that losing her to someone else would be unthinkable.

Colt pulled the collar of his coat up over his ears and tossed a handful of potato chips onto the rough water. Our feathered traveling companions screeched loudly and dove for the chips before they sank below the surface and became fish food.

Colt grinned back at me. "I think if we covered this boat with barbecue potato chips and cheese curls, we'd be more popular with the birds than any trawler carrying fish."

My brother walked over and stood next to me at the railing. I swept my binoculars around once. The sea was empty. Most of the fishing boats were farther out, and the incoming storm had kept pleasure boats docked. "Shitty weather, eh?" he said.

"Yep." I lowered the binoculars but still kept a watchful eye on the water. We'd been making these drops for nearly two years and had only run into problems twice. Once there was a pleasure yacht that seemed to be following us, but it'd turned out they were behind us to find out where the good fishing spots were. It was pretty fucking funny considering we were a fishing trawler heading away from the best fishing grounds. Another run-in with the coast guard was definitely less funny. As they pulled up to find out why the fuck we were floating away from the fishing grounds and why our nets were still stacked, Slade came out of the pilot house with an old coffee can. He told them that we were out at sea to distribute our dear father's ashes, his last wish. Colt and I had been floored and duly impressed with his quick thinking. Slade had even shocked himself. It had worked. The coast guard gave us their condolences and motored away from our boat and our illegal cargo.

"If you don't mind me pointing this out, bro, you seem to be in an ugly fucking mood today," Colt said.

"I do mind, so fuck off and keep watch off the starboard side. Something has me uneasy today, and I don't know why."

Colt shoved some chips into his mouth and turned around to lean against the railing and watch over the starboard side. "Probably just the weather. And the fact that Rincon sent us this drop order just an hour ahead of time. What the hell is going on with him?"

"Like everyone else— it's greed."

"Yeah, I guess so. I hear things are a little messy between you and Street, huh?"

I didn't answer. Colt knew damn well that meant I wasn't interested in the topic, but apparently, he was feeling immortal today.

He crunched on another chip. "I think you're going to regret this."

I lifted the binoculars to my face. "Just because you like playing house doesn't mean it's right for me. Street knows that, and if she can't understand then I guess there's not much to say. I don't need any ball and chain around my nuts."

He laughed. "Ball and chain? Shit, if that's what I've got around mine by being with Jade then I'm happy to keep them securely locked up. One thing I know for sure— if you lose Amy for good, you're going to get even grumpier and then I won't even want to be around you."

"Scary threat. Now go tell Slade I can see them in the distance."

He pushed off the railing but stayed next to me.

"Don't want to hear any fucking more, Colt."

"Right." He took a step and stopped. He really had gotten up feeling invincible this morning. "Everyone in the entire fucking town knows how you feel about Amy. Shit, guys won't even step within ten feet of her because of you. The only person who doesn't know how you feel about her— is you. Pretty fucking thick— that head of yours."

"Colt— swear to God, I'm gonna—"

"Yeah, yeah, I'm leaving."

I pushed Colt's irritating lecture out of my head for now. I still wasn't feeling right about this morning, and I needed to focus on the drop. A feathery fog had fallen over the sea, but I could see our contact boat anchored in the distance. Ace, our main contact, had seemed pretty fucking shady at first. He'd always insisted on holding a gun to one of our heads, in case something was wrong or short with the cargo. Not that we had anything to do with the quality or quantity of the goods we were delivering, but Ace seemed to think it was a necessary threat for Rincon to keep up his end of the deal and think twice about cheating him. The funny thing about that was that Rincon couldn't have cared less about us. If one of us had our head shot off, he'd just find a replacement crew. There were plenty of people willing to take a risk to make a quick buck. Coincidentally enough, when Jade's creepy ex, Ray Ward, had put up a reward to find her, Ace had answered the call and provided Ward with information leading to Jade. Only once Ward lured Jade back by holding Colt hostage, he'd decided not to pay Ace the reward. A big mistake. Ace had helped us get Jade back from Ward, and after that, we'd gained a mutual respect for each other. Now the drops were much less intense. Until today.

Ace climbed down into the inflatable with his two men. Occasionally, he brought different men with him. We never bothered to learn their names because it wasn't necessary. This was a business deal, not a tea party. Only one of the men with him looked familiar, he was an older guy with skin weathered by days at sea and a tattoo of a giant squid on his forearm. We'd always just referred to him as *squid*. There was something about the set of Ace's shoulders that didn't seem right. The man was as confident as a fucking rooster in a flock of horny hens, but today his rigid posture looked forced.

Colt leaned over the stern and lowered the rope ladder as the inflatable boat bobbed up and down over the uneven tide like a car on a roller coaster. Even with the battering the small boat was taking, Ace sat like a pillar of marble, smooth-faced and stiff.

As they made their way across, I lifted my binoculars and looked over at the other boat. As always, Ace had left two crew members behind. One was familiar, a goofy looking guy who always wore a yellow beanie pulled tight over long, dark hair. The other guy, who stood right next to yellow beanie, wasn't anyone I'd ever seen before. I knew Ace went through crew members pretty fast. He was quick to get rid of them if they lost their nerve easily or were unreliable, but this new crew overhaul seemed more than usual.

Ace's boat, a slick overhaul on a fast Sundancer, lifted up and down on the choppy current. Aside from Ace's unusually severe posture and the new crew members, everything seemed normal and quiet. But just as I lowered the binoculars, my eyes glimpsed something that shouldn't have been there. I lifted them again and focused on the Sundancer. From the corner of my eye, I could see Ace and his men getting closer to the *Durango*. I squinted through the binoculars and waited for the stern of Ace's boat to dip down with the rough sea. The bow went up and the wave rolled beneath it until the stern dropped. I hadn't been imagining it. There was a small motorboat tied off on the far side of the Sundancer.

Adrenaline pumped through me. As badly as I needed to jump into action, I couldn't let on that I knew something was up. Even though they were only twenty feet away, I casually swept my binoculars toward the inflatable boat. The man behind Ace had a gun in his back.

I held two fingers up to the pilot house, our signal to let the person in the captain's chair know that something was up. "Colt, be alert." That was our verbal cue to be ready to pull a gun.

I motioned for him to step back from the stern. I reached behind and pulled the gun out from under my shirt but kept it out of sight. Colt did the same. I glanced back to the pilot house. Slade was already coming down the steps. We hadn't had an incident like this yet while running cargo for Rincon, but we were ready and we knew how to avoid making things worse by looking alarmed or ready to fight.

I knew without looking back that Slade had positioned himself behind the nets near the cargo hold. One thing was for sure, I was already in a pissed off mood and these yahoos cutting into my work day and most importantly my profit was making my mood that much worse. My patience was thin, and I was ready to split some fucking skulls in two.

Ace's face was the first to peer over the stern. His new, unwanted sidekick was right behind, trying hard to keep his gun out of view. Ace shot Colt and I a look that let us know trouble was on the rope ladder behind him. I decided I didn't need more than one unwanted visitor on the *Durango*. It was time to pull the rip cord on this clumsy-ass heist.

As the guy was busy pulling himself over the side of the stern with one hand, while still trying to conceal his weapon, I stomped to the back of the boat, drew out my gun and leaned over. My hunch had been right. The second guy, squid, had just put his hands on the rope ladder. He had his gun still, which meant he'd double-crossed Ace. He was obviously even dumber than he looked.

"Permission to come aboard denied," I said as I pointed my Smith and Wesson directly at him. With a gun barrel staring straight at him, it took him a second to put together what I'd said. He retreated back into the inflatable while I kept my gun pointed at him.

Ace held up his hands. "Guess I don't need to tell you guys that this asshole behind me has a pistol jammed in my back." Ace looked at Colt and me, and the glint in his eyes told me that he trusted us to get him out of this mess and deal with the pirates any way we saw fit. And with my mood, that wouldn't be a problem.

The guy behind Ace glanced my direction. He looked uneasy but determined. "Let him come up or I put a bullet in this man," he snarled.

I shrugged. "Go ahead. He's nothing to us, and when your human shield falls to the ground, I'll have a clear shot at your head. Works for everyone." I motioned toward Ace. "Except him. Sorry, dude."

Ace nodded. "Nope, perfectly understandable. Just make sure to get a clean shot. I wouldn't want him to get away with just a massive brain injury or some bullshit like that."

Our casual, macabre conversation was making the fool with the gun more nervous. He shoved Ace forward with his pistol. "Then move toward the cargo hold. I'll collect what I came here for and be on my way."

Colt nodded slightly at Ace, letting him know he should move toward the cargo hold.

"Keep a gun on squid man down in the inflatable," I told Colt. He moved to the stern and I followed Ace and the gunman to the hold. In order to see down in the hatch, they had to circle around and stand directly in front of the nets, which was the plan.

"Open this up," the guy demanded. As I stepped forward, Slade walked out from behind his hiding spot. The deck creaked beneath Slade's feet just as he raised his gun arm. The gunman had better reflexes than I would have given him credit for, especially in his agitated state. He swung his arm and knocked Slade's gun clear. My brother was infamous for moving like fucking lightning in a brawl. He grabbed the man's shirt and shook him hard enough that the asshole stumbled back and fell into the nets. Somewhere in the stumble, his gun went off. The loud shot and the searing pain in my shoulder were almost simultaneous. I grabbed my arm. Blood trickled through my fingers, but I could tell instantly the bullet had only grazed me. Ace, no longer captive, swung around and kicked the man's arm so hard, I could hear the bones in his wrist crack. His gun bounced on the deck, and Slade grabbed it.

Colt was the first to notice that I'd been hit. "Hunter, what the hell?" He stared down at the puddle of blood on the deck.

"Just a flesh wound, I think."

"You're leaving a big mess on my clean deck." Slade walked toward me. "Guess I better check to see if you're going to live."

"Hey, Ace, do you care if I make your raft into Swiss cheese?" Colt called from the stern. "His buddy is heading back to your boat. It would be fun target practice."

Ace waved his hand. "Be my guest. I've got another one." With his attention diverted, the gunman took the opportunity to kick Ace's feet out from under him.

"I'm fucking done. Excuse me, while I escort this piece of shit off our boat." I strode right past Slade. Ace was just pushing to his feet with the same rage in his expression that I was feeling.

A rally of gunshots behind me told me Colt was shooting holes in the inflatable raft. The guy scooted back as if a man eating tiger was stomping toward him. His foot tangled in a net, and as he lost his balance, I grabbed him with both hands. He tried to beat off the hold I had on him, but it was a pretty pathetic attempt. My arm hurt like hell as I clutched the guy's shirt and dragged him across the deck. He fell to his knees and couldn't get his feet under him. He grabbed at my hand, but there was no fucking way he was going to free himself. My week had been shitty, and this guy had decided to jump aboard the wrong boat.

"No, wait, no" he pleaded like a worm on a hot, dry sidewalk. I lifted him up by his shirt collar and waistband and tossed him overboard. His arms and legs splayed out to the side like a flying squirrel, and he belly smacked the water with a grunt.

I turned around to my audience.

"Feel better now?" Colt asked.

"As a matter of fact, I do."

"Uh, except for that blood river pouring from your arm," Slade said. "Looks like you need some stitches to match the ones on the back of your head."

I looked at him. "And how do I explain it to the doctor?"

"Super glue." Ace walked over and looked through the hole on my shirt. "Yep, a little super glue will patch that gash right up."

"Yeah, I've heard of that too," Colt said.

"Great. As long as I get to take some good long whiffs of the stuff to give me a buzz and forget that glue is holding together my flesh, I'm all for it." I looked at Ace. "What the hell happened? Never would have expected you to end up in front of some two-bit pirate's gun."

"Let my guard down. Brick, the old guy with the squid tattoo, was working against me. Who knew he had those kind of balls?"

"Don't know if I'd call it balls or fucking stupidity," I said.

"They're clinging to the last bit of canvas," Colt called from the stern. "Their partner has already bailed. He's coming around on their speed boat to pick them up. Should I put some holes in the hull?"

I glanced around once with my binoculars. Aside from the clowns clinging to the deflated raft and their partner in his zippy little boat, we were still very much alone out on the water. "Go ahead."

"Wait." Ace walked over to Colt. "Allow me." He took hold of Colt's gun and fired several rounds. The guy ducked down as bullets pinged off the fiberglass hull. Ace fired straight at the outboard motor and it sputtered, smoked and died. He handed the gun back to Colt. "There, now I feel better too. Let's move this rust bucket closer to my boat so we can get on with our business."

"Hold on," I said. "First, since I'm going to be the one that has to deal with Rincon, why don't you tell me where the hell this all fell apart, eh?"

Ace looked pissed. "You accusing me of something, Stone?"

"Yeah, I guess I am. But I'm not accusing you of a double-cross. I'm accusing you of being fucking careless." I waved toward the small motorboat that was slowly taking on water even as its two frantic passengers were tossing the water out. "I mean, what the fuck? I'd heard you were moving on soon. Maybe you've already checked out of this job. If that's the case, then let someone who gives a fuck take your place. I don't want to run into this again."

Ace's face reddened as he walked closer to me, but he wisely kept himself out of range of my fist. Colt and Slade moved in on him, but I shot them a subtle shake of my head. I wasn't planning on this escalating. My arm was already numb from the bullet slicing me, and I didn't need anything else to add to the irritation. I just wanted some details to take back to Rincon.

"Stone, you know I like you, but don't push because I can push back hard."

"I just need to know what to tell Rincon when he asks." I relaxed my stance some, and it seemed to make him do the same.

"You want to know the truth," he said, "I think someone's playing dirty on his side. I always send him those coordinates at the last possible minute, and I'm the one that comes up with them. No one else on my side knows where the drop will be."

Yells from out on the water let us know that the small boat was slowly sinking. I looked over at Colt. "Get out the life vests."

Ace's brow creased. "What the hell? Are you going to save their sorry asses?"

"No need for them to drown. Just like us, they're trying to make a fast buck. I'm not letting them onboard though, and I'm using the vests as a lure."

Colt came back out with three life jackets. He and Slade had already figured out my plan. The three of us always thought the same when it came to shit like this. Slade grabbed a vest and held it out over the railing like bait for a hungry shark. "Here you go," he teased.

I looked down on the three fools who were now clinging to the side of their boat. The other side was completely submerged.

The one whose bullet had grazed my arm swam closer to the *Durango*. With a major dose of suspicion in his expression, he reached up to catch the vest. Slade let it dangle overhead.

Ace and I walked to the railing.

I looked down at the guy in the water. "Tell us who the turncoat is on Rincon's side, and we'll drop three vests down. You'll have a better chance of staying alive. Otherwise, the storm that's rolling in is going to take all of you out to sea and you'll be swimming in Davy Jones's locker in no time."

The guy stared up at me. "Fuck that. I can't tell you. It'll be the end of all of us."

Slade laughed. "I guess you pick your poison then. Either you become fish food or target practice for the guy you're protecting. Personally, I'd take my chances with the target practice. You're at least three miles from shore and swimming in this rough water will make it feel like ten. That is— if you even head off in the right direction."

Colt held out another vest. "Well, you going to talk?"

The guy was already getting tired just treading water for a few minutes. He had no chance without the vest. He looked back at his partners. They were in full panic mode as the last side of the boat started slipping below the surface.

"How do I know you're really going to drop those vests?" the guy asked.

"All I can give you is my word," I said. "Either way, you're screwed."

"I think I'll take my chances with the sharks." He turned to swim back toward his friends just as the boat took its last breath. The water churned into a whirlpool as the suction of the sinking boat drew it down. A hurricane of froth and bubbles followed. The three men were completely stranded in the storm current that grew worse with each passing minute.

"Shooting them all in the head would be the merciful thing to do," Ace suggested. "I'm glad to do it."

I stared at him. "Remind me never to cross the desert with you." I looked at my brothers. "Pull the vests out of view. One of them will crack for sure."

Slade and Colt pulled the vests back in.

"It was Nelson," one of them yelled from the water. "Nelson is behind it."

Colt shook his head. "Shit, Rincon's right hand man. It's always the last person you'd expect. I guess that's why it's best to work with your brothers."

I motioned for them to toss the vests over.

"I'd have let them drown," Ace said.

I nodded. "Yep, that's where you and I are different." I leaned over the railing. "See the way the tide sort of meets in a line right there." I pointed to the water. "The waves look like they're running into each other."

"Yeah, I see it," the guy said as he struggled to put on the vest.

"Follow it and you'll end up on land. And keep moving or you're done for." I straightened and looked over at Slade. "Let's get Ace and this cargo over to his boat. I'm finished with this fucking sea adventure."

NINE

AMY

I clutched the tiny square of paper in my hand as if it was the solution to all my problems. It wasn't, of course, but every time the doctor gave my mom some new meds to try or changed a dosage, it gave me a small sliver of hope that it would be the magic potion we were looking for. I'd considered the taping of the cupboards extreme until she'd made cookies with snail poison. While I hadn't given the doctor any of the truly alarming details of her last few episodes, I'd mentioned that I was concerned she was hearing voices more frequently and that I thought a medication adjustment was in order. He'd reluctantly written out a new prescription with the warning that it probably wouldn't help and might possibly make things worse. I had to promise that if things didn't work out with the new meds, I would bring her in for an evaluation to be placed in a hospital setting.

The only bright side of having to deal with some major Mom problems was that I hadn't had much time to think about Hunter. Not that I'd pushed him completely from my head but, for a change, he wasn't front and center.

The local coffee shop was right next to the pharmacy, and the obsessed coffee patrons had lined up to taste a free sample of some fancy, frothy new coffee drink. There was one parking spot left open. As I headed toward it, a shiny black convertible Jaguar with the top down and a surfboard jutting out the backseat came toward me. The guy behind the wheel had long sun-streaked hair, a typical surfer hairdo, and black Oakley sunglasses. Before I could turn my shabby little junkster into the spot, he swept in with his slick convertible. The surfboard loomed over the back of the car, seemingly laughing at me for losing the spot. But I wasn't in the mood to be ridiculed by a damn surfboard or have my spot snaked by a rich, salt-coated surf *dude*.

I threw my car in park and, piece of shit that it was, it choked and coughed and stalled. I didn't care. Surfer dude was just getting out of his fancy car as I climbed out of mine.

"Hey, Malibu," I called, "that was my damn parking spot."

He turned around. He'd pulled a shirt on over some nice muscles. His board shorts still looked wet. He pushed his sunglasses up on his head and looked at me in a way that made me feel as if I'd stepped out of the car in my underwear, and I didn't mind. He had nice blue eyes and a strong jaw. I was always a sucker for a strong jaw.

It might have been the Jaguar talking, but suddenly, a little voice in my head suggested I flash one of my famous, come hither smiles. It had been so long since I'd felt free to flirt, I'd almost forgotten how. But this guy didn't know me and he didn't know Hunter, and I was going to go for it.

I shoved my hands in my back pockets but brought my shoulders forward to push my somewhat underwhelming boobs into view. "I just think if you're going to snake a girl's parking spot, you should at least buy her a cup of coffee."

He stepped toward me, and he didn't lose any of his appeal on closer inspection. "I am sorry about that. I guess I didn't notice you." He looked down at my body and then back up at my face. "But I'm definitely noticing you now. And I think you're right. I owe you a cup of coffee." He glanced around the parking lot. "Looks like the free coffee offer is over and some spots are opening up. I'll go in and grab a table."

"Sounds good." I pointed back to my car. "I'll just go

park."

"I'm David, by the way." He reached out his hand. I shook it. "I'm Amy." He had a firm grip, but there was no exchange of those weird little electrical charges I always felt when Hunter touched me. I brushed that silly comparison from my head. If I wanted to try this, to be on my own to meet men and maybe even fall in love, I was going to have to stop measuring other men up against Hunter.

I parked and went into the pharmacy to turn in the prescription. I didn't want to appear too anxious for my coffee date. The pharmacist raised his fluffy gray brows as he read the doctor's writing. Never a good thing when a medication request made a pharmacist do a double-take.

I left the pharmacy wondering how on earth I could ever meet someone and bring them home to meet my family, a family that consisted of one loony woman who spent her entire day trying to keep out of the grasp of invisible aliens. Between my mom and my menacing neighbor, there was no way I could ever bring anyone home, or, for that matter, let anyone pick me up for a date. Pick me up for a date— what a foreign notion that was.

I headed toward the coffee shop. I was slightly nervous, and that really irritated me. No big deal, Amy. A nice looking surfer with a spiffy, expensive car asked you to sit and have coffee. He was probably going to turn out to be a jerk anyhow. I seemed to be a magnet for jerks, especially oversized, hard-edged ones. Once again I had to push Hunter from my head. The Stone brothers had sort of warped my view of the world, and of men in general, but I was ready to branch out. I'd just be myself, and if that didn't fly, too bad. I could always live without a guy.

David waved to me from a table in the back corner. He leaned back and watched me walk toward him with an appreciative grin. He was smooth. I wasn't completely sure I liked *smooth*. In truth, I wasn't sure I even knew what I liked.

I sat down at the table across from him.

"I'll go up and order our coffees," he said. "What would you like?"

"A coffee mocha with whipped cream and an extra shot of chocolate. Oh, and see if they'll put in a drizzle of caramel."

He smiled. "Got it. Although it sounds more like an ice cream sundae than a coffee."

"Trust me, if they had any ice cream behind that counter, I'd be asking for a scoop of that too."

Stupidly, I looked around to make sure no one who knew me or Hunter was in the shop. I'd had to drive to a neighboring town to get to a pharmacy that stocked the medication my mom needed, so I was out of Stone range. I relaxed back in the chair and decided to stop being so damn paranoid. Otherwise, I'd eventually be standing in an apron next to my mom making suspicious tasting cookies.

David was tall and nice looking, not Stone brother handsome, but then few were. But this guy might have had enough more gentleman-like qualities to make up for it. Maybe it was time to move away from the Neanderthal type and onto something a little more evolved. That thought made me smile.

David returned to the table with the coffee. He pointed to my cup. "Took the liberty of having some cocoa powder sprinkled on top. Thought you might appreciate it."

"Good call. I like your way of thinking."

"What were you smiling about just a second ago? Looked like something amused you."

I picked up the cup and cradled it in my hands. "Guess I was just thinking how nice it was to have a good-looking guy bring me a cup of coffee."

"Uh, I hate to break it to you, but that thing you're holding stopped being coffee three caramel squirts ago."

I laughed. "Guess I do sort of order coffee that a ten-year-old might like."

He took a drink from his cup and leaned back. "Actually, it's refreshing not having my date order a cup of hot water with a side of lemon."

I laughed again. "So, is that what this is? A date? I thought it was an apology for taking my parking spot."

"I think this transitioned from an apology to a date when I watched you walk into this place and thought— holy hell, when did this angel land on earth."

I shook my head with a smile. "O.K., that line just had more sugar than this cup of coffee."

"Too much?"

I pinched my fingers together. "Little bit. Listen, you don't have to try so hard. My usual male companions think 'hey, get me a fucking beer from the fridge' is a term of endearment." I stuck the tiny stirrer into my cup and scooped up some whipped cream. He watched with great interest as I licked it off the stirrer. Apparently, I still knew how to flirt, after all. Of course, whipped cream was always a good tool for drawing in a guy's attention.

"So, there is a male *companion*? Actually, you said companions, didn't you?"

I took a sip of my extra sweet drink and twisted my lips. "Wow, that almost makes my teeth hurt. My kind of coffee." I'd avoided his question, but he seemed to be waiting for a response. It was a question that sort of hurt my head just thinking about. I'd been so damn attached to Hunter and his brothers, that it was hard not bringing them up in every conversation. "My neighbors," I finally blurted. Sometimes in my own mind it was just easier to talk about Hunter as my neighbor rather than as the person I was more connected to than anyone else on the planet, my own mom, included. "We all grew up together." I shrugged to assure him that they were nothing more than acquaintances. It was sort of like saying my nose was just the center point of my face, but I was going to have to stop thinking about Hunter. And dismissing him as unimportant was the first idea I'd come up with in a pinch. The last thing I'd expected on my way to getting my mom's drugs was to meet a hot guy and have to discuss my personal life.

"Good to hear." David seemed genuinely relieved. Or at least I convinced myself of it. Free coffee samples dispersed, the crowd in the coffee shop dwindled to just a few people working on computers and a couple of women who looked as if they could be sisters.

I glanced out toward the parking lot. The pale green surfboard jutted up over the expensive car. I motioned toward the window with my head. "Now that you know a little bit about me." I lifted my drink. "Like the fact that I have a monstrous sweet tooth, and I live next to guys with caveman manners, and that overdone compliments make me cringe— tell me a little about you."

"What would you like to know?"

"Well, you can start by explaining the really weird inconsistency of a man with a wax-covered surfboard and salt-faded board shorts driving a sleek, black Jaguar. Shouldn't you be driving a beat up jeep or something?"

"I like to head to the waves in style. I make good money, and you only live once. Besides, the Jag helps get girls." He swirled his cup around and took a drink. "I mean would you be sitting here having coffee with me if I'd just climbed out of a run-down jeep?"

"Actually, I would. Let's just say you sort of drove into my parking spot at just the right time. I needed this. And this." I lifted my coffee. "Thanks, by the way."

His phone buzzed. "Excuse me." He took it out and checked it. I was sure a guy like him had to get a flurry of phone messages and texts from girls. Or maybe I was just so used to it with Hunter, I assumed it was the case with any guy. Ugh, Hunter again. In my head, this was turning out to be one of those lame dates where the one person spends the entire night talking about their ex. At least the conversation was only going on in my mind, otherwise this man would have walked off with his coffee long ago. And I didn't want him to walk away. In fact, I hoped he'd ask for my number.

"Where were we?" he asked as he stuck the phone back in his pocket. "Oh, that's right, my unusual beach bum mobile. I guess I like nice things."

"What do you do, if you don't mind me asking?"

He paused. A pause when answering a pretty

simple question was never a great thing. "I'm self-employed. I'm in import and export."

A short laugh spurted from my lips. He looked slightly insulted. "Import and export?" I repeated. "Isn't that the default answer for people who don't want to go into the sketchy details of their shady side business?" Sometimes my straightforward tongue shot out ahead of my brain. I wanted to retract the question the second it'd left my mouth.

He took a long, slow sip of his coffee, and I was sure I'd just ended our coffee date. He stared at me over the rim of the cup and then lowered it to the table. "Or, I could actually be in import and export."

"You're right. That was bitchy of me. Sorry. I think I'm getting a sugar rush and then my mouth just sort of runs off with itself." I took another drink to shut myself up.

David checked his expensive looking watch. "Speaking of business, I've got to meet some people."

I'd blown it. My big mouth had pushed this one away.

He tossed me his napkin. I instinctively touched my mouth to see if I had whipped cream on my lips. He smiled. "It's not for your face. I was hoping you'd write down your phone number."

This time I paused. I was leaving my cocoon, and I

wasn't completely sure how I was going to adapt out in the real world.

"Of course, if you don't want to—"

"No, I do." I shuffled through my purse and found an eyeliner pencil. "This is the extent of my writing utensils." I quickly jotted down my cell phone number and pushed the napkin back over to him.

He picked it up and put it in his pocket. "I should get going."

"Yeah, me too. I've got to get ready for work."

"And what is it you do?"

I sighed wishing I had something exciting to tell him. But I made good money, and Jack had me practically running Lazy Daze. I needed to remind myself that I'd done pretty well. "I serve drinks and help run Lazy Daze. It's a bar off the highway."

"Yes, I know the place. Do you live nearby?"

"Yep. I live in Trayton. I have to admit, as a teenager I was always itching to get away from it, but now I'm not sure I'd ever want to leave the place. It's small and everyone has their noses in everyone's business and sometimes the smell of the ocean and the fishing boats makes everything you eat smell like fish, but in the morning, after the fog lifts and the view over the ocean stretches on forever, it makes you feel like you're living on the edge of the world. You know? Damn, I'm rambling." I looked into my empty cup. "And I don't have any more coffee in my cup to shut me up."

He was listening to every word. I wasn't used to it. I liked it. "You're not rambling, and I'm enjoying it. Best conversation I've had in a long time. And I do know what you mean. I love the ocean. I guess that's obvious." He stood up. "I'll walk you to your car, if you don't mind."

We walked outside. The late afternoon breeze had brought a clammy cold with it. I pulled up the hood of my sweatshirt. We reached my car. I smiled up at him from around the edge of my hood. "Thanks for the coffee."

He reached up and pushed the hood back off my head and pressed his hand against my waist as he lowered his face to mine. It was a nice kiss, nothing earth shattering but I hadn't really expected it. "I'll talk to you soon, Amy."

He headed back to his car. I climbed into mine and watched him in the rearview mirror as he pulled his phone out before getting into his car. He drove off. I lifted my face toward the mirror and touched my lips. I couldn't remember the last time I'd kissed someone other than Hunter. David's kiss had been fine, but it was just that, a kiss, two mouths pressing together. When Hunter kissed me, it felt as if my core was melting and turning every part of me into Jell-o. Damn. I was doing it again. I had to stop.

My phone rang as I started the car. It wasn't a number I recognized. With my mom, I always expected the worst. "Hello."

"There's this great seafood restaurant about an hour up the coast. Tomorrow night around seven?"

"Wow, I guess I won't have to waste any time in the next few days wondering if the new guy is going to call."

"When I see something I want, I don't believe in wasting time. So, what about the dinner?"

"I just happen to have tomorrow night off. So yes." It felt so strange making plans with another man. I wasn't sure if my heart was beating so hard because I was excited or scared. A little of both, it seemed.

"Just text me your address, and I'll pick you up at seven."

My heart fell to my stomach. There was no way I could let this guy come to my shabby house where masking tape was dangling off kitchen cupboards and weeds choked the front path. And Hunter. What if Hunter was home when David came to pick me up? I'd made it clear that I wanted to see other guys, but I had no idea how that little plan was sitting with my oversized, overprotective neighbor. "Uh, I'll meet you here again. I've got to pick up the prescription I dropped off.

It won't be ready until tomorrow after five. It's for my mom's arthritis," I added unnecessarily.

"All right. See you tomorrow night, Amy."

"Bye." I hung up. Today, I was Amy and not Street. It felt weird and sort of lonely to hear my real name, instead of my nickname. Not completely sure I was ever going to get used to that.

TEN

HUNTER

Rincon was out by his pool, a massive rock-bordered stretch of turquoise water that looked as if it was spilling off the side of the cliff that his house sat on. His usual bevy of half naked, beautiful female guests were draped in tantalizing positions across the chaise lounges and pool floats.

Slade groaned inwardly as he gazed out at the number of naked tits bobbing in the heated pool. The air temperature was a tad cold for a day by the pool, but the sun was out and Rincon had had a lot of heat lamps installed to make the area around the pool feel like a damn tropical island. Perpetual summer was what he'd instructed his landscape architect to give him. Rincon had told me his theory that keeping his yard in everlasting summer meant everlasting bikini season. Guess that's why he was making the big bucks.

"When I die, I want my ashes spread out over this pool area," Slade said.

Normally we both looked forward to a quick visit with Rincon. It always meant expensive booze, good weed, a line or two of coke and, of course, the likely event of a raunchy fuck with one of his pretty pool partners. But today, I wasn't in the mood for any of it. Yesterday's drop had not gone smoothly, and Rincon would have to be told that his closest partner had betrayed him.

Several of the girls noticed us walk in. "Hey, Stoney hunks," Bridget, a spunky blonde with gigantic fake tits, said with a wave of her hand. "Haven't seen you boys in awhile."

Rincon leaned forward out of the shade of an umbrella and pushed his sunglasses up on his head. "Hunter, Slade, got your message that you needed to see me. Come on over and get some lines before Penelope and Chloe snort it by themselves." He smacked Penelope on the ass as she leaned over the small table. She shrieked and nearly blew away the white powder but then quickly licked her finger to clean up the mess from the table. She rubbed it on her gums.

Rincon waved them away. As they sashayed past, Choe made a point of rubbing against me. Penelope was a little more forward. She reached down and brushed her hand across Slade's fly.

"If you're going to tease me like that, sweetie, you better expect me to follow-up with my own tease," Slade said.

"Oh, I'm always ready for you." She pursed her lips and blew a kiss at him before strolling away. He shot me a pleading look, but he knew we had business with Rincon. And it wasn't pretty business. The last thing I needed was him wandering off with Penelope while I broke the news.

I hated having to be the one to tell him. We'd been on shaky ground lately. But it had to be done. I didn't give a damn about the rich asshole stretched out on the lounge. It was for our own safety. Even though we were all grown up, I still hadn't gotten past the idea that I was the big brother and I had to protect Slade and Colt.

I didn't see Nelson's big head anywhere around. "Hey, do you think we could go inside?" I asked. I wasn't about to tell him with all his party buddies hanging within earshot.

"Sounds important," he said with a smirk, a smirk I would have liked to have wiped off his face. He leaned over and snorted two lines of coke and reluctantly got up from the lounge.

We followed him into his living room. One entire wall was glass windows, giving you an uninterrupted view of the ocean from any place in the room. Rincon liked to strut around like a rich fucker, as if he'd earned all the money himself. But I knew his father had been a stock broker who died from an alcohol soaked liver. He'd left behind a small fortune, and Rincon was really good at spending it.

He sat on his white leather couch and motioned for us to sit.

"We're not going to be here long," I said remaining on my feet. Slade propped himself up on one of the stools sitting in front of the wet bar.

"You should stay. The women won't forgive me if I let the infamous Stone brothers slip out of reach." He leaned back. "Where's the third musketeer today?"

"He didn't come with us." I grabbed a cigarette out of my pocket and held it up to ask permission to light it. Because Amy had always been bugging me about it, I'd cut my habit down to three smokes a day, but right now, I needed something to take the edge off. Hell, with the week I'd been having, I was surprised I wasn't back up to two packs a day.

"Go ahead."

I lit it and took a long drag. "Don't know if you heard but the drop yesterday didn't go too well."

He'd been leaning casually back against the seat as if he wasn't really interested in anything I had to say, but now I had his attention. "What do you mean? The deal was completed. I got the payment."

"Yeah, it was completed after we fought off the guys who showed up to steal the cargo."

"Why the hell am I just hearing about this now?"

I shrugged and took another hit. "Where's your man, Nelson? He'd know."

"What do you mean? I haven't seen Nelson since yesterday morning."

"You mean your contact on the other side didn't mention it?" Slade asked.

"Not a fucking word." He pulled his phone out.

"Wait," I stopped him before his finger pushed the button. "They probably didn't know. I doubt Ace even told them. It would make him look bad. Besides, we already found out where the problem started."

Rincon lowered his phone. "You did?"

I glanced back at Slade and then turned back to Rincon. "Your buddy, Nelson, is double-crossing you. The men who showed up told us they got the coordinates from Nelson. He was part of it."

Rincon stiffened, then an unexpected laugh shot from his mouth. "Impossible. I don't know who these clowns were or how you extracted this supposed information, but you're wrong."

"Figured that'd be your response. Someone who

knew the coordinates was in on this. Ace was the only person who knew on the other side."

His jaw tensed with anger as he got up and walked to his bar. He poured himself a shot and then smacked the glass hard on the granite counter. "I'll talk to him later. Damn, and my day started out so well, but now it's turned to shit."

"Sorry about that. We can see ourselves out. But next time, no one knows the coordinates but you. Otherwise, you'll need to find yourself another boat." I motioned for Slade to follow me. He looked longingly out at the pool.

"Next time you come, plan to stay longer," Rincon said. "The girls will be pissed that you left so soon."

Slade shot me another pleading look like a kid being dragged out of the pet store where they're giving out free puppies.

"Yep, next time," I answered. My disappointed brother plodded behind.

We got out to his car and climbed inside. "Don't know why we couldn't have stuck around for awhile." Slade slammed the car door hard. "A week ago you would have been the first to suggest it. This thing with Street has you walking around with your underwear jammed up your crack."

"What the hell are you talking about? She's got

nothing to do with this. Just didn't feel like hanging out there."

"Yeah, right. Nothing to do with it." He turned the car around and headed down the steep driveway. "You need to take a good long look in the mirror, bro, and see just how twisted up you get when Street's not around. Reflect, buddy. Reflect on your reflection."

I looked over at him and took another hit on my cigarette. "Reflect on my reflection? Thank you, Dr. Phil, for that brilliant fucking suggestion." I leaned forward and cranked the radio. Led Zeppelin blasted through the speakers. Of course it was *the* song.

Slade laughed and pointed at the radio. "Hey, it's the song about the street corner girl. I guess even the damn radio is trying to tell you something."

I slumped down in the seat. "Just drive."

ELEVEN

AMY

I turned the corner toward home. The usual blanket of fog wasn't hanging over the town but the moon was nonexistent. It was hard to see where the sea ended and the coast began. Most of the houses were dark. Our neighbors were quiet, keep-to-themselves types and most liked to look the other direction when it came to the two shabby houses in the center of the block. I suspected that had more to do with the people living in the houses than the overgrown front yards and peeling paint. They'd also looked the other way when the houses weren't so rundown and the brothers were struggling to survive a horrible childhood. When I was younger, my mom would stop and talk to neighbors on her stroll to the mailbox or picking up the paper, but that had stopped long ago when she'd decided everyone was out to get her.

Our television flickered through the broken blinds on the front window. The new medication was making her sleep a lot, and I was actually thankful for that. She couldn't tape up the house or hit people with vases or poison her only kid with cookies when she was sleeping.

Tonight had been my third date with David. The first dinner had gone all right, but he'd seemed preoccupied by something and I wasn't feeling myself either. Our conversation hadn't flowed like it had in the coffee shop, and I was still being constantly plagued with the stupid habit of mentally comparing David to Hunter. David was always coming up on the short side of the comparison.

Tonight, we'd given it another try. As usual, he'd been a perfect gentleman, something I wasn't used to. So far, he'd only kissed me and taken hold of my hand. Tonight, he'd picked me up after my shift at Lazy Daze. We drove to the beach with a blanket and bottle of wine. We talked awhile and kissed a lot, but I wasn't ready for anything else. David had accepted that with some disappointment. But he'd kissed me goodnight and told me he wanted to see me again.

My head was swirling like fudge ripple ice cream when it came to David. One minute I thought he might be someone I could fall for, and the next, I was telling myself to end it before things got deeper.

Hunter's motorcycle was in the driveway, but the house was dark. I had a strange, very fleeting desire to talk to him about this new situation with David. Hunter was the person I always went to when I needed to talk. Jade was fairly new in my life and our friendship had been sealed almost immediately. Still, there was only one person who I'd always told all my deepest secrets and feelings to and that was Hunter. He knew me better than anyone, and while he wasn't always the best listener or advisor, I had always counted on him to be there for me. I smiled at the idea of discussing my newest dilemma with him.

I saw the tiny red glow of a cigarette or joint on his front porch as I pulled into my driveway. The giant silhouette sitting on the front porch was easy to recognize. No one else had shoulders that nearly spanned the entire top step. Immediately, my pulse raced. That alone might have been the reason I was so on the fence about David. He hadn't made my pulse race or my knees weaken or even my hands tremble, physical reactions I always had when I saw Hunter.

I stepped out of the car on jelly knees. His handsome face was halfway hidden by the shadows of the porch, but I could tell he was looking at me. We hadn't spoken in a week and everything about that felt wrong, almost as if I hadn't taken a decent breath for seven days.

"You're out late," he said.

The sound of his voice caught me off guard. It was a sound that could leave me breathless or filled with heartbreak. I willed my feet forward. "And you're in early." I pushed out my most casual tone but just having to *push* it, made it sound completely forced.

I sat on the porch next to him, took hold of the joint and stuck it between my lips. He stared out at the street. It seemed he was straining not to turn and look at me.

"Jade said you met someone."

"Huh. Did not expect you to lead with that." I handed him back his joint.

"Seemed like a good topic."

Jade had a theory that the only thing Hunter needed was a little shove, and she was sure me dating another guy would do the trick. But I wasn't at all convinced she was right. "Guess I was tired of going in circles, chasing my tail like a puppy."

He nodded, but I could feel the tension radiating off his body. Apparently he was having a hard time trying to act casual too. "I made no promises. Not saying that this isn't twisting me up inside, Street. Cuz it is."

A rare confession of feelings from Hunter was hard

won, and this one was particularly hard because I missed him badly. Not talking to him for a week was sucking the wind from me. Talking to him now was keeping me just as breathless.

"Who is he?"

A dry laugh shot from my mouth. "Should I write down his address so you can go stand on his porch and glower at him?"

"Nope, just making sure you're not hanging out with a bad element." A smile turned up the corner of his mouth. "But I guess just about anyone who isn't me is a step in the right direction." He extinguished the joint on the porch step. "Just want to make sure you're safe, Amy. Old habits die hard."

"Tell me about it." I tossed my keys on my palms, weighing just how much I wanted to tell him. "He's got money, but I'm not sure what his business is. Just like I have no real idea what you and your brothers are doing. All I know is he treats me well." I looked over at him. His profile with his straight nose and long dark lashes was always heartbreaking. It somehow made him look more innocent, hiding all the ugliness he'd been through. "He treats me like I matter."

He faced me. His eyes flickered with something, an emotion that I'd rarely seen in his expression. "Don't fucking sit here and pretend you don't matter to me, Street. Just don't."

I wrapped my arms around my knees to hold myself tighter. There was no damn way I was going to cry in front of him. We both fell silent.

I looked out at the other houses with their neatly trimmed lawns and thoughtfully planted hedges. It was no wonder everyone looked the other way. "Sometimes I think our crappy childhoods stunted our growth. Our asshole fathers are gone, but they both still have control of us. We never grew past what happened in these houses. We never allowed ourselves to say— hey I survived and dad is gone and good fucking riddance."

Hunter stared down at the ground. "Sometimes the memories are so tightly wound around my throat, I can't even take a decent breath. Colt, Slade and I were living in hell."

"And I wasn't? Sure, my dad wasn't nearly the monster that yours was, but he was pretty fucking low on the fatherly love scale. So don't try to bottom out your upbringing, Hunter, because I'm still dealing with my fun." I waved toward my dark, pathetic little house where my mom slept in her drug stupor.

He reached back to the cut on his head. "Yep, the stitches in my head remind me of that."

"Didn't you go back to the doctor to get them cut out?"

"Nah. Slade's going to cut them out tomorrow."

I remembered, then, about an unexplained wound

on his arm that Jade had mentioned. I could still see the gauze under his shirt. "What happened to your arm?"

"It was nothing. Something that happened on the job."

"The job. Right."

"See. I live a sketchy life. That's why I'm not worth the bother."

I shook my head. "Hang on while I go get my violin, Mr. Woe is me." I released my legs and leaned my hands back behind me. "I've decided I'm done being held hostage by my past. I'm going to clean up my house, maybe paint it, and I've decided to have someone fix the engine on my dad's boat."

"Why? Are you going to start fishing?"

I rolled my eyes. "I can sell it and use the money to fix up the house. My dad left us with some bitter memories, but he also left us with a house and boat. I'm moving on."

"With some guy who has cash in his pocket and treats you well."

"Nope, I'm moving on alone, and if I find a nice guy in the meantime then that will be the frosting on top." I stood up. "I've been waiting for—"

He gazed up at me, and I lost the words for a second. It was him. I'd been waiting for him to come around. But he hadn't.

The light on our front porch turned on. My mom was up. I stood up, but before I could walk away, he took hold of my hand.

I couldn't bring myself to look down at him as he gripped my hand. Or as he spoke. "I'm not going to lie, Street. Nothing is right without you. Feels like the ground beneath my feet is giving way, but—" His words were interrupted by the squeak of his front door.

A tall brunette walked out dressed in just a t-shirt and panties. I was pretty sure her name was Shelly, but I didn't care enough to puzzle it out. "Hunter," she said sweetly, "aren't you coming back to bed?"

Now I turned to face him. He kept a grip on my hand and stared up at me as if a half-dressed girl hadn't just asked him to return to bed. I yanked my hand free and ran across the weed covered yard to my house.

As I put my foot on the first step, our screen door popped open.

"Off my porch!" I heard my mom's voice but didn't see the garden shovel until it glinted in the light. As I covered my head to block the end of the shovel, I squeezed my eyes shut to brace for the imminent blast of pain. But it didn't come. Heavy footsteps pounded the wood steps and a thudding sound followed.

"It's your daughter, you fucking loon. It's Amy," Hunter yelled over my mom's hysterical cries.

I lowered my arm and lifted my face. Hunter had hold of the shovel, and he held my mom's arm. Mom stared at me for a second as if she was trying to figure out why I looked familiar. Her eyes were glazed and unfocused from the medication.

"Amy, my god." She sobbed, covered her face and ran back inside.

Hunter's chest rose and fell with deep breaths. I glanced back to his house. He'd crossed the space between our houses as if he had rockets on his feet. His visitor was still standing on the porch. She'd witnessed the whole embarrassing episode.

Hunter lowered the shovel and reached for my face. But I stepped back. The last thing I needed was to feel his touch. He looked at my front door and then at me. "Fuck, Amy, you've got to—"

I held up my hand to stop him. "No, don't Hunter. I don't want to hear this tonight. She's just on new meds is all. They always take awhile for her to get used to." I was holding it together, but it was an act. Inside, I was ripping apart. "Go back to your slumber party."

He stood there towering over me and staring down at me as if I'd just pulled out any final strings still holding his stony heart in place. Then he stomped down the steps and swung the shovel at our tree, hitting it hard enough to wedge the metal end into the trunk. I turned around and went inside.

My mom had climbed into bed and had already fallen back asleep. I went down the hall to my room, shut the door and slid to the floor. I wrapped my arms around my legs, pulled my knees closer and cried.

TWELVE

HUNTER

Slade and Colt were already sitting in our usual booth when I walked through the door at Lazy Daze. I didn't see Amy, but her car was in the lot. It had been three days since our conversation on the porch. Shelly had stepped out to interrupt and remind Amy that I was a complete asshole. Not that she ever needed reminding about that.

We hadn't gone on a job in a few days. The *boss* was dealing with shuffling in new people and getting rid of old, namely Nelson, his ex-right hand man. While we waited for our next job, I'd carried my tools down to Amy's father's boat. She'd mentioned wanting to fix it up, and working on engines was the one thing that could keep my mind out of the black hole that kept wanting to swallow it. The hard, cold reality was that I missed Amy so much it hurt. I shifted between wishing I'd been a real guy with a real job and a future and wanting to fall into an abyss and get sucked down into hell where I belonged. It was the darkest my mood had been since I was fourteen. Back then, my dad had beaten me so badly, I'd actually plotted how I might kill him. It had only ever been a fantasy, a macabre plan that had him in the bathtub with me tossing in a radio or hairdryer, something that would fry him up good. It'd been one of the darkest periods in a life that had never seen too much light.

Slade and Colt were staring at me as I slid into the booth. "Shit, is my hair on fire or something?" I asked.

Slade grinned at Colt before turning to me. "No. But it might be soon."

Jade came over with a beer and tequila shot. "Thought you might need this."

"Yeah? If you say so." I threw the tequila back. All three of them were staring at me. Amy came out of the office. She wasn't wearing her apron and had put on the green, curve-hugging dress I'd always loved, a dress that I'd nearly ripped off of her more than once. She glanced our direction and paled the second she saw me.

"What the fuck is going on?" I reached up to my head. "Did I forget to tuck my horns in? Or are all of you just nuts?"

Jade looked at Colt. "You didn't tell him?"

Colt lifted his hands in surrender. "You didn't give me time."

Jade scurried away as if I really had sprouted horns. I took a long drink of beer. Something told me I was going to need it. I slammed the mug hard on the table. "One of you asswipes should tell me what the fuck is going on."

Slade leaned forward with a small, almost gleeful smile as if whatever was happening was entertaining to him. "Well, brother dearest, it seems Amy's new boyfriend is coming to pick her up here. She's off for the night, and they're going out— on a date," he added unnecessarily and with another heap of glee.

Colt looked over at him. "Fuck, Slade, should I get you a tub of popcorn? You look excited like you're about to settle down to a good movie."

"What can I say? It's boring here tonight. No hot single girls and the beer is sort of flat. But now my big brother has walked in to provide some entertainment."

Colt turned to me. "Seriously, bro, maybe you should just head back out. Thought you were going to play poker tonight."

"It got cancelled." I stared across the room at Amy. She was trying her hardest not to look my direction.

Colt elbowed me. "Might be better if you take off, don't you think?"

I was trying to tamp down my anger and figure out

what the hell I was going to do. The thought of Amy with another guy wasn't just a suggestion, an irritating idea that I kept brushing out of my head to keep from going fucking nuts. It was a real thing, and the real guy was coming to meet her. And I had only myself to blame. I moved to slide out of the booth, thinking I needed to go somewhere else and get fucking plastered.

"What the hell? Why is Rincon here?" Slade asked.

I looked across the room. "What the fuck?" I got up and walked toward him. Colt and Slade followed. Our deliberate movement across the bar made every other patron sit up and take notice. They knew that trouble usually followed when the three Stone brothers moved in one direction together.

Rincon's mouth dropped open when he caught sight of us. He looked equally shocked to see us. He was dressed up as if he was off to an expensive nightclub or snob-filled party. He glanced around almost nervously as if we were the last people he wanted to meet in a public place. This particular public place wasn't exactly his style either.

"So, *this* is your usual haunt?" Rincon asked. He nodded as he took in the shabby decor and faded leather seating. "Guess that makes sense."

"Maybe you should explain why you're here," Colt said.

"Don't worry, boys, not here to tread on your territory. I'm just here to pick up my date." He leaned to the right and looked past me. "And there she is now."

We all turned.

Amy was walking toward us looking as if she might fall down in a dead faint. Even her lips were white. "What are you guys doing?" she asked all of us but looked straight at me. "This is my date. Remember," she said pointedly to me. "Please, Hunter." Her voice had dropped to a whisper.

Rincon looked confused. "You know these guys?"

"Yes, they're my neighbors."

Rincon nodded. "Ahh, the neighbors." He laughed. I'd always fucking hated his laugh, but now I just wanted to smother it with my fist. "I never would have guessed. Well, Amy, we should get going. The club gets really crowded after midnight."

Amy pulled her pleading gaze from my face and smiled weakly at Rincon. "I'll just get my coat."

I grabbed her arm. "Yes, I will help you get your coat. Excuse us," I said without making eye contact with Rincon. Amy stumbled along next to me, having to take two steps to match every one of mine.

We got to the office, and I slammed the door shut. Amy swung around to face me. The color had returned to her face, and it was the color of rage. "We had a fucking deal. You were going to look the other way when I started dating someone."

"Don't know where the fuck I was when this deal was made, and looking the other way isn't going to happen, especially when you've hooked up with a guy like Rincon."

"What? You mean rich, nice looking, well-mannered?"

"No, I mean a fucking drug dealer."

Some of the color left her cheeks again. "How do you know that? You're just making that up because you're pissed." She shoved her small hands at my chest and tried to slide past me, but I caught both her wrists.

She blinked back some tears as she glared up at me. "You're either in my life one hundred percent, or you're out of it . . . completely. I can't stand this anymore."

"His money comes from running cocaine over the water."

Again she tried to free herself.

"I know this because we're the boat running his cargo. Colt, Slade and I are his crew."

She blinked up at me, looking surprised and hurt. I swallowed the dry ache in my throat.

"Fuck," she said with sad surrender. "I just can't win." A tear fell down her cheek. The sight of it made my chest sink as if a pallet of bricks had dropped on it. I released her wrist and went to wipe the tear with my thumb.

She slapped my hand away. "No, you don't get to do

that. You don't get to do shit that just makes my heart ache more." Another tear fell. It was killing me to watch. "You don't get to be nice at a time when I'm trying my hardest to hate you." She punched my chest, and a sob bubbled from her lips. "You don't get to do that." She fell against my chest. I wrapped my arms around her.

Her shoulders shook a few times. Then she sucked in a shaky, deep breath. "The worst part of everything always going to shit," she muttered without pulling her face from my chest, "is that I can't even go to my best friend about it. Because he's a big part of everything going to shit." She looked up at me. "There needs to be two of you. Then I can stay mad at one of you and talk to the other about how I'm mad at you."

I smiled. "Trust me, the last thing this town needs is two Hunter Stones."

There was a sharp knock on the door. "Amy," Rincon called.

She stepped out of my arms. "I'm going to go out with him, Hunter. I need this. For the first time ever I feel like I'm part of the real world, not just the little sheltered world I built between my house and yours. And oddly enough, since you work for him, it seems I've finally found someone who you can't intimidate."

Rincon opened the door. He shot me an angry scowl. "What's going on, Stone?"

I shook my head. "Nothing, just a little *neighborly*

chat." I stepped aside. It felt as if I was digging my heart out of my chest and handing it to the asshole.

He held his hand out for Amy. She hesitated before taking it.

I kept my arms straight down at my sides. My fists were tight as steel as they walked out.

THIRTEEN

AMY

My mom had gone in to take another nap. I knew now what it was like to be a young mom with a toddler relieved when the baby finally laid down for a nap. Mom's meds were too heavy. With the exception of the violent shovel attack on the front porch, she'd been a walking zombie, barely able to speak or think. There was obviously a fine line between manic episodes and a comatose state, a line that would allow her to function, but we hadn't found it yet. We were going to cut back on the dose, and as always, it was just wait and see. It was hard to wait and see when you had no idea what you were waiting for.

The weather was cooperating completely with my plan to clean up the front yard. A thin spray of crisp, salty air flowed over the yard, and the sun above was just warm enough to let me work without a cumbersome jacket. I had gone to the hardware store to get gloves, weeding tools, a rake and a box of trash bags.

Hunter's bike wasn't in the driveway. It was too early for him to be up and off. Chances were, he was sleeping in some girl's bed and he hadn't dragged his ass home yet. There was movement inside the house though, which meant that Slade was up. He cranked on the radio, and I decided music might make the work go a little faster. I ran up their steps and walked inside.

Slade heard me and came around the corner of the kitchen. "Street"—he looked past me—"Are you alone?"

"Uh, yeah. Who should I be with?"

"No one. I just thought maybe Hunter was with you. I haven't seen him since he stomped out of Lazy Daze last night." He leaned against the doorjamb. "So, how was your date? Still can't fucking believe you're hanging out with Rincon."

"Yep, I seem to be a magnet for trouble. And about the date— don't ask. Having your brother drag me into the office for one of his nosy ass reprimands and lectures was the highlight of the evening. Everything went downhill from there. I won't be seeing that guy again. He's not who I thought he was."

"No? That's good cuz he's pretty fucking sketch."

"Said the guy who works for him."

"Good point. But we're just middlemen. So that

makes us only semi-sketch. What are you up to?" He looked pointedly at the work gloves sticking out from the pocket of my jeans.

"I'm doing some yard work, and I figured I could filch off of your music supply. My mom took the batteries out of my radio. She was sure they were radioactive." I walked over and opened the front window. "This place needs airing out anyhow. Smells like you guys are using dirty shoes as air freshener."

"Yeah, that would be the kitchen." He lifted a hand before I could make the obvious suggestion. "I was just about to tackle cleaning it. That's why I cranked the music. Thought it would make the job easier."

"Yep, me too. Just to let you know, I'm going to make my yard all shiny and spectacular. So your house is really going to look like shit. You might want to come out and pull some weeds. You know how neighbors talk."

He laughed. "That they do. And they'd run out of topics fast if they didn't have us to talk about."

Jade pulled up just as I stepped back outside. She carried out two big cups and handed me one. "Strawberry mango smoothie. My treat. As long as you fill me in on all the details of your date."

"O.K." I quickly took a long sip. "There, it's mine now. The date details are so uninspiring, I figured you might want to take the smoothie back after you hear them." I walked over to the porch and pulled out the gloves I'd bought her. "This is really nice of you to come help."

She put down the drink on the porch step and pulled on the unwieldy canvas gloves. "I needed to get out. Colt is working on the siding, and there's no way to sit in the house when he's hammering on the outside."

"Wow, we're just all a bunch of do-it-yourself home fixer upper people. Like a damn cable show." I pulled out a trash bag and gave it a shake like a sheet coming out of the dryer. "I figured we'd start over there pulling weeds and work our way to this side."

"Quite an elaborate plan of action." Jade took several sips of her smoothie and sighed. "There, I'm ready to go." We walked to the far corner near our mailbox and where my mom used to plant daisies in spring. It had been so long since there'd been flowers there, I almost wondered if I'd just imagined the tradition.

Jade glanced over at the Stone house. "Maybe if we have some energy we can tackle that jungle too. It's pretty darn ugly on that side. I don't see Hunter or Slade coming out anytime today to join in on the weed pulling party. Even if they are providing us with some tunes."

"Hunter is MIA and Slade is inside tackling the kitchen disaster."

She laughed. "Slade washing dishes. I'll have to sneak in there and snap a picture of that."

"Well, he doesn't always wash them. I've caught him just throwing away the ones that would take too much scrubbing. Pretty soon they'll be down to just a couple of plates and a glass or two."

We dropped to our knees and began the task of yanking weeds. Some had been growing for a long time, and they had roots that were as long and sturdy as a tree's.

"You said Hunter was MIA? He marched out of Lazy Daze last night like he was going to start walking and not stop until he'd circled the entire world." Jade pulled a weed and plucked off a ladybug before shoving the weed into the trash bag. She stopped and looked at me. "Colt told me how they knew the guy. Did you know what they were up to when they went off on their boat?"

"No. I knew they weren't out fishing, but I tried not to think about what they might be up to. Wasn't it just typical of me to latch onto another upstanding citizen like David Rincon?"

"Colt and I got into a little fight about it last night, but he insists they're trying to save up enough so they can start doing something else, something that doesn't have the threat of jail time hanging over it."

"That would be good." I yanked out a particularly stubborn weed and realized the entire root ball was left behind in the dry ground. "Do you think it'll grow right back if I leave behind the roots?"

"I think that if there is a nuclear end to the world, the only things that will survive are weeds, cockroaches and Skittles. So, yes, I think that same weed will be back tomorrow." She reached behind us for a forklike tool. "I think this will help you dig down to the roots."

I stabbed it into the ground. "This is more therapeutic than I expected. You know, the brothers were pretty young when their dad died. While it was better that he was gone, it also left them to fend for themselves at a pretty young age. None of them did too well in school. They were all smart, but they were much more street wise than book wise. It's not too surprising that they ended up working for someone like David. I just hope they can find their way in this world before any of them ends up hurt or in jail . . . or worse. I know Colt is on a much better path now that you're in his life."

She smiled. Jade was one of the prettiest girls I'd ever met, and when she smiled, she looked almost unreal. Colt had been a hard nut to crack when it came to girls. He'd always been such a town heartthrob, he hadn't ever needed to bother with any serious relationship. None of the Stone brothers had to try too hard when it came to women. Their rough childhood had made *relationship* a dirty word. Jade was the one to finally break Colt's shell, and you only had to spend a short time with her to know why. She'd had her own stretch of an ugly past and had turned out pretty spectacularly in spite of it.

"What happened last night on the date? He's certainly a nice looking guy, even if he is a drug dealer."

"God, when you say it like that, I just want to kick myself. I thought he was too good to be true. He took me to this ritzy, members only nightclub. Took us about an hour to get there. First there was an awkward grilling session about my relationship with the Stone brothers and in particular, Hunter. I guess the scene of Hunter dragging me through the bar and into the office didn't escape David's notice."

Jade laughed. "Nope. The entire bar saw that little show."

"Great. Then he spent the rest of the ride talking on the phone. I was pretty pissed by the time we reached the club. Turns out he had a bunch of his friends meeting him there. Lots of pretty, fake eyelash and boob type girls. You know, just the type I love to hang with."

She laughed. "I see where this is going."

"Yep. The polite but cool and rich surfer dude suddenly became the smarmy, polished coke dealer. Didn't like his friends at all and they seemed even less impressed by me. We couldn't really find anything to talk about. By the end of the evening, we both knew that it was over. Not that it had ever really started."

We scooted to the next section of yard.

"So my first venture out into the world of life after Hunter was a disaster." I yanked another weed and an ugly beetle-like bug came crawling up from the dirt. We both screamed and jumped to our feet. We stared at the little beast as it hurried to burrow itself back into the dirt.

I glanced around at the crop of spindly weeds still surrounding us. "I think I need some more smoothie. It's going to be a long day."

FOURTEEN

HUNTER

It felt as if I'd been up for three straight days. Not counting the few pass out sessions on Fletch's flea ridden couch, it had probably been close to that. The cards were starting to look like a red and black blur. Lack of sleep and lots of party treats in the form of alcohol, weed and blow were making my head feel as if it was filled with helium. But the pile of money in front of me was enough to keep me semi-alert. Or at least alert enough to win round after round of poker.

Two nights ago, I'd walked out of Lazy Daze determined to wallow in a pool of pity. Fletch had called to let me know that the poker game was back on. I headed straight to the game, figuring my luck couldn't get any worse. And it didn't. I'd managed to win a cool pile of dough and pushed the idea of Amy dating Rincon out of my head. I knew the relief was temporary, but the booze and coke had cooled the rage. The adrenaline rush I'd gotten from seeing Rincon walk out with Amy had, apparently, given me an edge in poker. I had no idea why, but I was playing like a fucking poker gladiator. Fletch had folded hours ago, and Sully had stomped off in his usual spoiled princess fit after losing his ass.

This would be my last round. I hadn't been home in three days, and my phone had died long ago. The last two players stared at me over the tops of their cards. Their eyes were bloodshot and angry. I'd only just met them when we all sat down to play two nights ago. They'd lost plenty, and they were now eyeing me with a lot of hatred and plenty of suspicion. The one guy, Mack, was butt ugly with tiny scars all over his face as if he'd either gone through a major bout of chicken pox as a kid or had someone spray his face with a pellet gun. His friend, Deke, had a black beard that he pulled and twisted every time he had a good hand. Didn't matter how good his poker face was, that beard gave away his hand every fucking time.

My poker fairy godmother hadn't left my shoulder yet. I had an Ace high flush, so my money pile wasn't going anywhere. The guy with the pitted face folded with a pair of twos. His friend grinned. He'd been twirling his beard into a black icicle, so I figured he was holding something decent. He laid down three of a kind.

I fanned out my flush and reached forward to sweep the pot toward me.

"Fucking cheater," Deke snarled.

"Didn't cheat. Just played a lot better than you two clowns."

The lack of sleep, loss of money and final comment was all they needed. Deke scrambled like a rabid dog over the table. Empty beer bottles clattered together like bowling pins as he tipped the table over. I backed my chair out of the way, and Deke fell face first onto the floor. The cards and my money cascaded down behind him. Mack took the easier route. He circled around the upturned table. He lunged for me, but I threw my fist into his face, surprising the hell out of myself with how sharp my reflexes still were. He flew back with a bloody nose.

Fletch came out of the bedroom rubbing his fat belly and squinting into the light. "Christ, Stone, what have you done now?"

"Wasn't me. Got some sore losers here."

Fletch's eyes rounded. "Watch it!"

I turned around as Deke hit me with a beer bottle. I ducked but caught it on my cheekbone.

I reached up. Warm blood seeped from the gash it'd left behind. "You fuckface, I won that money fairly and now I'm done." His face blanched white as I reached for him. I grabbed the front of his shirt and pounded my fist into his face. The guy was limp in my grasp when Fletch finally stopped me from delivering another blow.

"Stone, stop. You're going to kill him." It took me a few seconds to comprehend his words. The haze in my head was growing thicker by the second. I dropped my hold on Deke, and he crumpled to the ground.

The knuckles on my right hand were swollen and covered with blood. His and mine. I stumbled over to the kitchen sink and splashed my face over and over again with cold water. Mack recovered first. He grabbed his half conscious friend off the floor and pulled his arm over his shoulder. He snarled something angrily at Fletch.

Fletch held up his hands. "Hey, don't blame me. You two were stupid enough to call him a cheater and then fly over the table at him. Way I see it, you're lucky to be walking out of here." They stumbled out the door, and Fletch locked it behind them.

He looked at me. "You can't seriously be thinking of riding home tonight."

I walked out of the kitchen. The light in the room pulsed overhead making my head hurt. I leaned down and swept up my money. My right hand was nearly numb from pounding the guy. "Yep. I'm just going to step into your shower for a few minutes to wake myself up and then I'm out of here. My brothers are probably wondering what the hell happened to me." I righted the table and helped him pick up the beer bottles. I shoved the wad of money into my pocket. "Thanks for inviting me to the game."

"Anytime, buddy. Hey, there are some bandages in the medicine cabinet. You might want to try and close that cut up. Looks deep."

I walked into the bathroom and undressed. Blood was still oozing from the gash on my cheek. It was going to leave a scar for sure. I had to turn at an angle to fit in the small shower stall, but once I'd found the right position, the water felt fucking nice as it poured down over me. I'd taken my mind off everything for a few days, and it had helped. But now I was heading back home, and home meant I'd see Amy and that meant feeling like someone had stomped on my chest all over again.

FIFTEEN

AMY

I passed my mom's room on tiptoes, but the floorboards creaked anyway. "Amy, is that you?" she called. A loud sniffle followed. She'd been crying off and on since she'd come at me with a shovel. I'd told her over and over again it was the meds that'd caused her to do it, but that provided little comfort.

I popped my head into her room. She sat hunched under my old, faded flamingo patterned beach towel. I wasn't completely sure when and how beach towels became her suit of armor, her protection against all the aliens trying to get her, but if it worked to make her a little less paranoid, then I wasn't going to question it. She hadn't touched the bowl of soup I'd brought her for dinner. Her shoulders looked ridiculously thin, like a metal hanger holding up her sweater and her beach towel cape.

"Mom, I told you, you need to eat with this medication."

She blew her nose on her tissue. "Can't eat because the medication is making me nauseous. Guess those brilliant doctors didn't think about that."

"I think food will make you feel better, in every way." I knew my words were drifting right past her. Her complexion was sallow beneath the dim light in her room and her dark eyes looked as if they'd sunk into her face even more, as if they were going to eventually be swallowed up for good.

I'd been putting off telling her about the doctor's appointment I'd made for her. It was always better if I told her just before it was time for her to get dressed and go. Then she didn't have days to think and stress about it. I needed to get her help before I lost her for good. These new meds were only making everything worse. She wasn't hunkering around corners with vases anymore, but she had been brought so low by the chemicals in her bloodstream, I was sure she'd been thinking about suicide.

"Mom, can I get you anything? I'm just going to pop over next door and talk to Slade." It was just after midnight, and I'd been in bed when I heard Slade pull into his driveway. Hunter hadn't been home for three days. Slade had driven to his favorite pool hall to see if anyone had seen him.

"No, I'm fine. I'm tired. I think I'll rest." She scooted down and pulled the towel over her.

I headed out the door and across the yard. I'd been making good progress with the weeds and mess, but my worry about Hunter had slowed me down some. The light was on in the kitchen. I walked inside.

Slade was getting a beer out of the refrigerator. The Stone brothers weren't big on showing emotion, but his face was smooth with worry.

"Did you hear anything?" I asked.

He pulled out a chair and shook his head. "No one had seen him at the pool hall in the last few days. Don't worry," he told me, but his tone wasn't too convincing. "He's a big guy who can handle himself better than anyone. I haven't heard from the cops or a hospital, so that's a good thing."

I sat across from him.

"He'll be home soon, Street. And then I'm going to kick his ass for doing this. I'm sure he's with those bikers he's been hanging with lately. I don't know much about them except the one guy is called Fletch. They're big into poker, and you know how Hunter likes to play cards and make wagers."

"Yeah." My stomach was twisting into a hard knot. So many ugly scenarios were dashing around my head.

"This was my fault." My throat constricted around the words. "I shouldn't have gone off with David that night. Hunter was really upset."

"No, Street, don't do that to yourself. What you're doing is good. You need to show Hunter that he's not being fair to you." It was rare to have a serious conversation with Slade but, of all the brothers, he always made the most sense. Maybe it was the middle brother thing. Not that he hadn't lived through just as much despair as Hunter and Colt. He had. He just seemed to have come out of it a little more grounded.

"Right now, I don't even care what he's done in the past," I said. "I just want his ass home and safe. And I'm going to be right there when you kick his ass for doing this."

We both fell silent and thought about the comical scenario of someone trying to kick Hunter Stone's ass. Slade was the first to break the silence with a laugh. "Yeah, me and what fucking army, eh? It always sounds easy when the big goof isn't around." His phone buzzed, and we both jumped. Slade looked at his phone and shook his head to let me know it wasn't Hunter.

I slumped back against the chair.

"Hey, Rooney, what the hell are you doing up and about this late?" Slade asked. He sat forward. "Really?"

I tapped the table to find out what was going on.

Slade lifted the phone from his mouth. "Rooney said

there's a light on in the *Durango's* pilot house." He placed the phone back. "I'll head down there right now." Rooney was a guy we'd gone to school with. His father owned three fishing trawlers, and they were moored near the *Durango*.

"What?" Slade asked. "It is? That fucker, we haven't seen him in days."

This time I reached across and tapped his arm. He held up a hand to hold me off a second. "Rooney, can you do me a favor? Walk down to the *Durango* and see if the big dick is up there. Call me right back. Thanks man, I owe you." He hung up.

"Hunter's motorcycle is parked down by the marina. I don't know what the hell is up with him. Asshole." His phone rang again. "It's Rooney." He pressed it against his ear. "Is he there?" He paused. "You dickwad, where the hell have you been?"

It was Hunter on the other end. I relaxed back and tamped down the tears of relief that badly wanted to spill.

"Are you coming home? You sound like shit." Slade listened. I could hear Hunter's voice through the phone, but I couldn't make out the words. They sounded slow and deep.

Slade rolled his eyes at something Hunter said. "Yeah, all right. You had everyone worried, fool. Yep, I guess I won't start selling off your stuff yet. Later." He hung up. "He's been playing poker for three days. Sounds like he's been living on whiskey, weed and blow and nothing else. He says the sea air is making him feel better." He looked at me. "Not going to lie, Street. He's been on a downward spiral and—"

"And I helped start it." I finished for him. I got up and zipped up my sweatshirt. "I'm going down to the marina to check on him."

"Might be a good idea."

I walked out of the kitchen.

"And smack him upside his head for me, would ya?" Slade called.

I laughed. "Aren't you the brave one?"

I went inside my house and peeked into my mom's room. She was fast asleep, snoring softly from beneath the flamingo beach towel. I grabbed my keys and climbed into my car. The wave of relief I felt after finding out that Hunter was safe assured me that as hard as I'd been trying to break free from him, I was still just as attached as ever. There'd been too much time and shit between us. Somehow, just being friends didn't seem like an option. Our relationship was a giant, tangled ball of feelings. But I wasn't going to sort it out tonight or anytime soon. I just needed to see him. Horrible scenarios had been bouncing through my head for the past few days, and I couldn't sleep easy until I saw for myself that he was all right.

SIXTEEN
HUNTER

Hair of the dog wasn't helping me as much as I hoped. By the time I got back to Trayton, I felt as if I'd been chewed up and spit out. I headed straight to the *Durango*, thinking the cold sea air would be better than our stuffy house. And, somehow, it was going to be easier not seeing Amy's house or her shabby little car or anything else that might remind me how much I missed her. It was like walking around with a cold hard fist in my stomach, and I had no clue what to do about it. The more I thought about us together, the more I convinced myself she needed more. She was like fucking perfection, put on this earth to absorb some of the unwanted darkness. Having her living just a few yards away had made our lives better. She had been the one bright spot in our grim existence. She needed someone who deserved her. That sure as hell wasn't me.

I held the whiskey bottle to my mouth and lifted it straight up to get the last drops. The liquid burned going down, and the alcohol was no longer having much effect. I let the bottle dangle from my fingers. Leaning forward to put it down on the floor was going to take more energy than I had. I'd expected to climb up to the pilot house and collapse into a long winter nap like a goddamn hibernating bear, but instead, my mind was spinning. I seemed to have reached that point of being so tired, I couldn't rest my head enough to sleep. My mom used to call it the sleepy-crazies. She never had it easy. Aside from having to dodge my dad's iron fist, she had to deal with three wild, out-of-control boys. Guess that's why she eventually took the easy way out.

I yanked off my shirt and leaned my back against the cool plaster wall as I stared out the front windows of the pilot house. The moon added a strip of gold to an otherwise black sea. The rhythmic, lonely clanging of the pulleys and chains dangling from masts made the marina feel extra deserted. I felt as empty as the dock.

A shadow passed outside, but I dismissed it, figuring my lack of sleep was bringing on hallucinations. Then the door to the pilot house opened. "Shit, Slade, I told you I was fi—"

Amy stepped inside. The small lantern that hung on

a hook near the door swung back and forth, casting shadows across her pretty face and making her hair shine like copper.

"Well, damn." My words were stretched and slurred. "They sent an angel down to pick me up and take me to eternity. And here I thought I was going a different route."

She walked closer. I looked her up and down.

"If I knew angels were going to be this hot, I would have drank myself to death long ago."

She reached down and took the whiskey bottle from my fingers and put it on the floor. "I have about as much chance of being an angel as you have of meeting one as you leave this world."

She pushed between my knees and stood in front of me. The willowy soft scent that always surrounded her floated over me, making some of the ache in my head and chest lift away. She reached forward and pressed her finger near the gash on my cheek. The blood had dried, but one long yawn would get it flowing again.

"Why the hell do you always have to walk around with big gaping cuts? Can't you ever just go out and come back the same way you left?" She walked over to the captain's chair and leaned down into the compartment that held the first aid box. I watched her. My sleep deprived mind seemed to be making everything move in slow motion, and her long, graceful movements were causing the air to stick in my lungs.

She turned around with the first aid box and walked back. She sat on the bench next to me. Her body brushed my arm as she reached up with some antiseptic soaked cotton. I winced as she pressed the stinging solution against the cut.

"Does it hurt?" she asked.

"Little bit."

"Good."

"Street, I—"

"Shh. No talking. When you talk, it fucks things up. So, just shut up and let me take care of you."

"I'm O.K. with—

She pressed her finger against my mouth. "You're still talking."

"I was just—"

She sighed. "Oh my god. Nothing. Not a word."

I leaned my head back against the wall and closed my eyes. She pressed a long bandage over the cut. Having her so close was sending my body and pulse into overdrive. I hadn't been with her since the night in the office, and I ached for her now. She was my one constant. She was the only thing that still always made sense, and having her warm body brush up against my arm as she cleaned the gash reminded me just what a fucking drug she was for me. There was nothing I craved more than Amy, and it had been a long, harsh stretch of withdrawals. But I'd blown it with her so often, she had no reason to give me what I wanted most, her silky, naked body in my arms.

She stood up and returned the first aid kit to the compartment. Then she walked back and stood in front of me with an admonishing look. I was sure I was going to get a lecture for disappearing and not calling. Instead, she unzipped her sweatshirt and pulled it off. She dropped it on the floor. She gazed down at me, her bottom lip looking just a bit angry, as she reached down and grabbed the hem of her shirt. She lifted it up and off and dropped it to the floor.

The air that had been squeezed tight in my chest rolled out in a long shuddering breath. I gazed up at her as she reached back and unclasped her bra. It fell to the ground and the round, white breasts and rose colored nipples that I knew so well pointed at me. My cock was tight as granite as she unbuttoned her fly. I watched and swallowed hard with anticipation as she pushed her pants and panties to the ground. She stepped out of them.

I'd seen her naked so many times, but I couldn't take my eyes off of her. "I take it all back. You'd put angels to shame. Come here, my Street Corner Girl. I need you more than I've ever needed anything in my life."

She straddled my lap, and I wrapped my arms around her.

"I just need to feel you in my arms. Baby, I—"

She lifted my face. "Shh," she whispered. Her lips pressed against mine. Then with quiet, deliberate movements she kissed my nose, the tender skin above the bandaged cut, my eyebrow and my forehead. She was in control, and I was fine with that tonight. I was bone weary, and my heart ached so badly for the girl sitting on my lap that I could feel the pain all the way down my arms and legs.

As I smoothed my hands over her skin, it warmed my fingers and sent my pulse racing. I had to hold back. Tired as I was, if I didn't check myself, if I didn't tamp down my almost explosive urge to take her, to pull her under me, naked and open, then I would ruin this whole thing. And I was fucking things up too much lately.

She bit her bottom lip as she reached down and worked open the buttons on my fly. Her small hand slid down my pants. I pulled in a breath as her long fingers wrapped around my cock. It strained against her grasp as she stroked along its hard length.

She hopped off long enough to shimmy my jeans down to my knees. She swung her long, sleek thigh over my lap. Her long lashes fluttered as she stared down at my chest, running her fingers along the edges of my tattoos and up over the scars on my shoulders, scars left behind by an angry, sharp belt buckle. Her hard nipples rubbed against my chest as she leaned forward and kissed the ridges of the scars.

"We're not Hunter and Amy tonight." Her warm, sweet breath caressed my skin as she spoke. "No history, no pain or heartache, no anger, just two people whose bodies were made for each other." She rose up on her knees, reached between her legs and took hold of my cock. She slid down over it, her head rolling back as if drunk from the feel of it. "Just two people made for each other," she whispered as she lowered herself down.

She was slick and hot as my cock impaled her. Her arms wrapped around my head and she pulled my face against her. My tongue traced circles around her nipples as she pressed her perfect, round tits against my mouth. I gripped her ass as she moved up and down over me. We were one body connected at the core. It had always been like that with Amy. I'd always felt it with her. It was that strong, almost raw feeling that we belonged to each other that always scared the shit out of me.

"Oh, Hunter," she moaned as she squeezed her thighs and tightened her pussy, milking my cock with each movement. She ground her clit against me as she writhed faster and harder on my lap. I met her hungry pussy with hard thrusts, filling her deeper each time. Her thin arms tightened around me, and she pulled my face against her naked breasts. "Yes! Fuck yes," she cried out. A long string of erotic sounds followed, pinging off the walls of the pilot house.

Her skin was flushed pink as she caught her breath and smiled down at me. She began moving wildly, lifting up and plunging her hot sheath down over my stiff cock. The bench creaked and wobbled against the wall as our movements sped up. I met her wet pussy each time, impaling her with a force that made her squeak with pleasure. Then my soggy head cleared and my fingers dug into her hips as my cock exploded, releasing my hot seed inside of her. "Fuck yeah, baby. I needed you tonight," I groaned. "I need you every night."

Her body relaxed, and she dropped her face down to my shoulder and gazed out the side window. I smoothed my palm over her naked back and held her tightly against me.

"I thought something had happened to you." Her voice sounded small in the empty pilot house. "I don't want anything to happen to you. I couldn't survive that."

"I'm sorry, baby. I was in a bad place and the poker game got started and I just shoved all the shit that was bothering me out of my head."

She lifted her face and kissed me. "Don't do it again, or Slade and I are going to kick your ass."

"Yeah? You and what army?" I kissed her again.

SEVENTEEN

AMY

I pulled the rake across the dry, empty yard, kicking up a respectable cloud of dust in my wake. There was no grass, only parched earth scarred by the weeds that had once covered it like a bristly green and brown rug. But even without a lawn, it looked surprisingly better. I'd already made arrangements for a landscaper to come and fix the sprinklers and plant grass seeds.

Hunter walked out onto his front porch, wearing a tight white t-shirt that seemed to be working overtime to contain the mass of muscles beneath it. Sometimes the man looked so ridiculously intimidating, it was a wonder that the crows and squirrels in his front yard didn't all flee for safety. He picked up his toolbox from the porch and walked down the steps.

Nothing had been settled or untangled after the

night in the pilot house. I still couldn't reason my own actions when I'd walked up there and nearly jumped naked into his lap. I'd been so damn relieved to see him back safe that everything else, the anger, the hurt, had all but vanished. I'd missed him so much, and he looked so miserable sitting there with his empty bottle of whiskey, dark expression and open gash, all I could think of doing was something to make him feel better.

There had been plenty of selfish motive too. Seeing him sit there without his shirt, looking irresistibly hot as usual, my body had reacted instantly. If nothing else, my physical desire for Hunter Stone never wavered. In a way, it was a curse because it seemed the best way to protect myself from heartbreak was to say no to him. But I hadn't found the self-discipline I needed to turn him away. For now, nothing had been resolved, but we were talking again. And I needed that. I needed him to still be a part of my life.

I watched him from beneath the wide brim of the straw hat I'd been wearing to keep the sun off my face. The weather had been unseasonably warm, but I loved it. It was always easier to coax myself outside into the yard when it wasn't shrouded by a layer of cold fog.

"Where are you headed to with your box of tools, Mr. Handyman?"

"Heard someone wanted to fix the engine on their boat." He lifted the wide brim of the hat to see my face.

"I don't have any work, and I can't sit around all day with Slade and play video games. He's annoying to play with because he's way better and he gloats like a fucking spoiled brat about it."

"In other words, you needed something to take your mind off wanting to throttle your brother?"

"Yeah, something like that." He glanced around at the yard. "Who knew there was a yard under all those weeds? Guess I need to do the same."

"Yep. You guys will be the only eyesore left when I get this place all spiffed up."

"Spiffed? See, that's what I missed the most. Your comical vocabulary."

"Really?" I pressed my boobs so that they jutted against the snug cotton fabric of my shirt. "You missed my comical vocabulary most of all?"

"Well, not the *most*." Not giving a damn that we were standing in the front yard, he reached over and pinched my nipple between his thumb and forefinger. I felt the pinch between my legs as if he'd reached down my shorts and stroked me. Time spent not touching each other had been like a long torture session for both of us.

He lowered his hand to his side.

"Why don't you boys have work?" I looked up at him. "It's not because of me giving David the boot, is it?"

He shrugged. "Might have something to do with it, but Rincon was having staff problems. He decided to shake up everything, including his crew on the water. He's laying low for awhile and then he's looking for new people."

"Good."

"Yeah, just wait until the three of us show up at your door needing to be fed."

"Considering that the three of you can consume more food than six normal human beings, that would be scary. As it is, we don't have much in the kitchen except poisoned cookies."

"Did you say poisoned cookies? What the hell, did Santa leave you a bucket of coal or what?"

"Don't ask. Just be glad that Mom only came after you with a vase." I glanced away to let him know this wasn't the time for advice about my mom. I motioned toward the toolbox. "Are you really going to fix the *Ranger's* engine?"

"If it's all right with the owner."

"Yeah, that'd be great. Are you walking down there?"

"Too hard to carry this on my bike. But I'll need the keys to the boat."

I walked over and rested my rake against the porch. "Be right back. I'll walk down there with you. I could use a break from yard work. Just let me check on my mom."

Mom was in my dad's old chair. She'd fallen asleep

watching her favorite soap opera. Oddly enough, as groggy and out of it as she'd been on the new meds, she always remembered exactly when to sit down for her show. She still knew exactly what was happening in the series.

I grabbed the boat keys from the drawer where we kept them. I tossed my hat on the kitchen chair, knowing that I'd be struggling to keep it on my head on the breezy walk down to the marina. It was silly, but I was excited, like a schoolgirl with a damn crush, about spending some time with Hunter. He was like that for me. As annoying as it was, I was never able to tamp down those same giddy feelings I got when I was going to see him.

I hopped down the steps, and we headed in the direction of the marina. "What will you guys do now? Hey, maybe we could fix up the *Ranger* and renew our dads' commercial fishing licenses. We could start a fleet of fishing boats," I suggested.

"Not sure if two trawlers, including one that might not even be seaworthy anymore, would make a fleet." Hunter combed his black hair back with his fingers. The fabric on his shirt was stretched so thin with the movement of his massive arm muscles, I could almost see his tattoos clearly through it. "Slade's the only one with fishing in his blood. I'm not sure what the hell to do. We've all managed to stash some cash away. Working for Rincon had its risks, but it also had its benefits."

"Like not having to work too hard for money?"

"Shit, Street, when you put it that way, makes me feel like a lazy ass loser."

"Does it? Then I phrased the question perfectly." Mrs. Grinwald's black and white cat, Tux, came out from behind the rose bushes in front of her house. I leaned over, and as usual, the cat snaked itself around my legs in a perfect figure eight, making sure to rub every inch of its head, body and tail against my jeans. I stroked his ears. "Tux, I think you just might have been a pair of socks in a former life." A bird skittered out from the bushes and pulled away the cat's attention.

Hunter had grown quiet. He stared straight ahead as we walked, and I took the opportunity to gaze at his profile. His cheek was healing. The cut had scabbed over. It would leave a scar, but at least he was able to move his face without it bleeding again.

"You never did tell me how you got that cut." I'd hurt his feelings with my earlier comment, so I decided to change subjects.

He shook his head, letting me know he didn't really want to go into detail. "Bad losers at a poker game," he finally muttered.

We walked on. Gunmetal gray seagulls coasted overhead on outstretched wings, waiting for something tasty to pop up above the water's surface. Most of the fishing boats and even some of the pleasure boats were out at sea. It was an exceptionally beautiful day, clear blue with white puffs of clouds and water that looked like green glass.

I took a deep breath. The pungent smell that was uniquely coastal filled my nose. "This is the kind of day where I wonder how anyone can live in a place where you can't see the ocean? How do people who live in the middle of the country, landlocked and miles away from the coast, stand it?"

"Don't know."

I grabbed his arm to stop him and circled around in front of him. "You're mad about what I said."

"No, I love being told I'm a loser. Especially coming from you."

I smiled up at him. "Especially coming from me? So, what I say means something?"

"Stop. You know damn well it does, Street."

I traced my fingers over the black ink I could see underneath the stretched white shirt. "Here's the thing—"

He sighed. "Here comes one of those infamous Street lectures—"

"Fuck you, and that's right, so listen. Your dad sucked. O.K. I didn't need to state the obvious, but it's my lead in. The one thing he did right was work hard. He was a good fisherman, and while that was the only thing about his entire existence that should have earned him a shred of respect, it's a fact. But you guys, you're all so much above him on the human chain that it's like you aren't even the same species. Hunter, don't let him be above you on that. Even if he is just a crappy, ugly memory, he doesn't deserve to be thought of as a man who worked harder than his sons."

Hunter gazed down at me with those brown eyes that could see right into my heart. I knew my words had reached him. His throat moved as he swallowed, almost as if he was swallowing back what I'd told him. "We should get going."

I put my hands on his chest to stop him from moving forward.

"At this pace, I won't have any light to work on the engine."

"Good." I pressed my body against his. "Do you have any gas in the *Durango*?"

"Some," he said almost as a question. "What do you have in mind?"

I rubbed my hip against his fly and wasn't disappointed to feel his cock hardening against me. "I was thinking, it's such a nice day, it would be a shame to waste. You know that quiet little place on the side of the marina where we used to go when we wanted to—"

He grabbed my hand and pulled me along to the marina. "I fucking missed you, my wild little Street Corner Girl."

EIGHTEEN
AMY

It was only a ten minute journey to the small indent along the coast, a section of land that was so thick with trees no cars or bikes could travel through it. It was a deserted, overgrown coastal forest. As kids, we sometimes rowed to it and went exploring. I'd gone there many times with the brothers. It had been a great place to get away from our parents.

In that short stretch of time on the water, Hunter and I hadn't been able to keep our hands off each other. He had to drive the boat, but he still managed to take off my shirt and jeans.

As warm as the day had been, it was still too wintry to be wearing just a bra and panties. I got up and grabbed a towel from the bench at the back of the pilot house.

Hunter looked over at me with disappointment as I pulled the towel around my shoulders. "What's the point of taking off your clothes if you're going to cover up?"

"It's cold. I need to be smothered by my big, hunky boat captain. Then I won't need the towel."

"Aye aye, mate." He maneuvered the *Durango* to a quiet section of water, out of view of any nearby roads or houses. He shut off the engine. The motor for the anchor chain rumbled beneath the deck.

He spun his captain's chair around. "You were saying something about the beautiful day?"

"I was."

"Well, all right then." He grabbed my hand and led me down the stairs to the deck. "Wait there." He walked to the stern and came back with a giant green tarp. He shook it out and lowered it onto the deck. Then he reached up and yanked the towel from my shoulders. The ocean breeze tickled my naked skin. I felt deliciously exposed standing on the middle of the boat on the wide open sea in nothing but a pair of panties and a bra.

Hunter leaned back and squinted at me. "Hmm, something's not right."

I looked down at my scantily clad body. "What do you mean?"

"Oh . . . I know what the problem is. You're not

naked enough." He reached behind me, and I nuzzled my face against his chest as he unclasped my bra. He dragged it off my shoulders. His thumb flicked over my hardened nipple. Instantly, I pushed my breast harder against his fingers. He teased my nipple as he reached down and pushed my panties to the ground.

"I seem to be the one who's always completely naked."

"What's your point?" He sat down on the tarp. I went to follow him, but he put up his hand to stop me. "Not yet. I was just thinking how fucking hot it is seeing you walk around this deck completely naked." He waved me on. "A little show please."

I strolled to the railing and leaned over, jutting my bottom out. I glanced back over my shoulder. "How's the view from down there?"

Hunter was leaning on his elbow staring straight at my naked ass. "Very nice but I think you need to part those legs just a bit."

I moved my feet apart and the breeze cooled the moisture that was already pooling between my legs.

An appreciative groan rolled up from his chest. "Yeah, baby, this is making me so fucking hard."

I turned around and walked to the stack of nets. I reached up and grabbed hold of the rough rope, keeping my hands stretched up high above me, pushing my breasts out. "I think you've caught something in your net, Captain."

He reached back and yanked off his t-shirt. I sucked in a breath as I watched him push off his jeans and boxer briefs. His cock was shiny with slick moisture as he stomped toward me. The deck of the boat shifted slightly beneath his heavy footsteps.

I squealed as he reached for me. My hands released the net, but he stretched them back up and made me take hold of the rope again. "You stay right where you are, my little captive." He pressed his mouth against mine and teased my lips open with his tongue. As he kissed me, he tucked his hand between my legs and his callused, thick fingers slid through the hot creamy folds of my pussy. The wanton feeling of standing naked out on the open sea being caressed by his hands and mouth and the warm strands of sun made the whole thing that much more erotic.

"God, Hunter, this is such a fucking turn on, I'm almost ready to come." I took a deep breath. "I want multiple orgasms today, please. You know how to make me come again and again. I want that today."

"Then let's get this party fucking started," he growled as he pushed his finger inside of me. He was so damn skilled and he knew my body and my desires so well, he never wasted any time or movement. Every touch had a reason. Every stroke hit the right spot. He even had pressure down to an art. His thumb massaged my clit just the way I loved, and in response, I tightened my thighs around his hand to hold him exactly where I wanted him. His free hand teased and played with my nipples as the hand squeezed between my legs brought me to a shuddering climax. As my body thrummed with the feel of it, he jammed his finger deeper stroking every intimate inch of me as my pussy hugged his hand.

Whimpering with the sheer satisfaction of it, I could no longer keep a grip on the net. I released my hold and dropped forward. He caught me. I laughed as he swept me up into his arms.

"Sure hope there are no boats out there with binoculars pointed this way."

"Let them look and be jealous that I have my arms filled with the sweetest little fuck on the ocean." He spun around once with me in his arms.

"Not sure how I feel about that title. And what about those rich playboys on their yachts with their supermodel girlfriends?"

"Nope, I still win. If you don't like that one— how about dirtiest little fuck?"

I hit his chest with my fist. "Ooh. I hate that. I might just wriggle back into my panties if you say that again."

He gazed down at me. "How about the wildest, hottest little fuck?"

"Getting closer, but I was thinking something more

like beautiful sex goddess or something along those lines."

A smile tilted his mouth. "How the hell do you do it?"

"Do what?"

"Make every fucking day better. You know something, Street, I'm not sure I'd ever drag my ass out of bed or out of the house if I didn't know there was a chance to see you."

I felt as if someone had pushed a tennis ball into my throat. I was thankful for the sea breeze. It dried my tears before they fell. Not that it would matter if he saw me cry. I was naked in his arms clinging to him as if he was the only person who mattered to me. He knew. Even without the tears, he knew how I felt about him.

He kissed me as he lowered me down onto the canvas he'd placed on the deck. It was stiff and scratchy.

"Not exactly a downy comforter," I said as he knelt down over me. I reached up and wrapped my hands around his neck and pulled his face down toward me. "But as long as I have my hunky sea captain to warm me up—"

I wrapped my legs around him as he pushed his long, hard cock into me. The sweet ache from my first orgasm was still there and an involuntary frisson of pleasure coursed through me as he filled me.

"Sweet, tight, hot, there's nothing as fucking perfect

as your pussy," he groaned against my mouth. He used one arm to raise himself up and keep from crushing me. His massive size and his stone chiseled shoulders and arms made me feel so slight and weak that the sheer difference between us should have been frightening. He had so much power over me physically that I should have felt terrified instead of thrilled.

He squeezed me just hard enough to remind me of that power. He pumped his cock into me, and I met each thrust, enthusiastically. "Come again for me, baby," he grunted. "I'm staying hard. I won't leave you until you come again. I want to feel your pussy squeeze down on my cock. Don't deny me that, Street." He kissed me hard on the mouth while still grinding into me. Suddenly, he grabbed hold of me and spun us both around. He was on his back and I was on top of him. I straddled my thighs over him and braced my hands against his chest as I slid down over him, taking in his cock with slow precision. His lids seemed to get heavier with each inch. With his black hair, dark eyes and unshaven jaw, he looked less a sea captain and more a pirate, a dangerous pirate, and every part of him thrilled me.

I leaned down over him and writhed over his cock as his big hands took hold of my ass. The ocean rolled beneath the *Durango's* deck, causing it to rise and fall along with my movements. He held me tight against him, and we moved in rhythm, like two people perfectly in tune with each other.

Then the sensation started deep inside, the tingling feeling that felt as if my pussy was closing up on itself to prepare for the coming explosion. My fingers dug into his hard arms and my hips moved feverishly, wanting to absorb everything he was giving.

He knew I was close. "That's it, baby, take it to the edge. Take me fucking with you." He tightened his ass to push his cock deeper inside of me and that was all I needed. Splinters of light flashed behind my eyes as my pussy convulsed around his cock. His iron grip tightened on my hips and he held me firm as he thrust into me, making my orgasm grow in intensity.

"Yes, fuuuck yes," I moaned.

A low, guttural sound rumbled deep in his throat and his body stiffened as he came.

The sea breeze felt almost cold on my flushed pink skin. A small shiver raced through me as my body temperature dropped and my pulse slowed. I climbed off of Hunter and stretched out next to him. He turned and wrapped me in his warmth.

"This was a good suggestion, my sex goddess."

"Uh huh, but don't overuse the sex goddess title. It should only be used at the height of passion or in really important times, like when a bunch of your usual groupies are hanging around you at a party. Then you can call me sex goddess." I grew quiet. My bringing up the other girls had sprinkled a bit of darkness on an otherwise great afternoon. But it was always there like an irritating fly at a barbecue, the notion of the other girls, or *them* as he called his other conquests.

"You know they don't mean a thing," he said quietly.

The seagulls had moved in on the boat, certain that we either had fish or some good snacks onboard. They screeched intermittently overhead. It had been a perfect afternoon, but I'd broken the bliss with my comment. I could never shake it, the heartbreak of knowing that Hunter was never going to be mine.

"Nothing is right without you, Street. Nothing. But I've got nothing to offer. You deserve so much—"

I sat up. "No. Stop. Shut up. Don't pull that I'm not worthy shit on me anymore." I took a deep breath. I was never going to forgive myself if I cried. "What kind of a diamond licking, designer fucking purse wearing princess do you take me for? I've grown up in a little house, just as shitty as yours, and with not much to my name except a car with an odometer that has already gone around twice, a fairly worthless state quarter collection and an autographed picture of Justin Timberlake. And since I bought the damn thing on Ebay when I was fifteen, I'm pretty sure it's a fake. So don't give me the not worthy crap, Hunter. Please."

I grabbed my panties and bra deciding this whole

rant would be a lot more respectable if I wasn't sitting naked in the middle of a fishing boat. "Yeah, it's nice to have a roof over my head. It's nice to have food in my belly. And I'll admit it's nice to be able to buy a cute pair of shoes occasionally, but I don't need much to be happy, Hunter. I just want to love the person I'm with and to have them love me back. I want to know that when things are tough and on days when the world is particularly ugly that the person I'm with will hold me and kiss me and tell me everything's going to be all right." A small waver in my voice warned me that tears could be imminent. "You've always been that person for me, Hunter. But lately it's not enough. Sometimes when you're not around, I feel empty. But it's not because I'm lonely, it's because deep down I feel like I'm chasing after something that isn't really there."

He sat up. His hair stood up in black spikes all over his head as he raked his fingers through it. He reached for his jeans and pulled out a joint. "I'm nothing without you, Amy, but you shine like a goddamn angel all on your own. The only thing I do is dim that light with my big, fucking shadow." He lit the joint and took a long hit. I waved it off when he offered it to me.

I hopped up and pulled on my jeans. He avoided looking up at me. "One day it will dawn on you that I'm gone, that your days aren't going to be lightened by your *goddamn angel* anymore, and you'll be sorry as hell."

His dark lashes still curtained his eyes. I couldn't see his expression, but I could see his Adam's apple move up and down his throat with a deep swallow. He took another hit of weed and extinguished the joint. We got dressed and climbed back up to the pilot house.

As hard as we tried to untangle this, the whole thing just kept getting more knotted.

NINETEEN

HUNTER

"I just realized something," Slade said as he lowered his beer glass to the table.

"This should be good," Colt said with a roll of his eyes.

"No really. I have no focal point. I'm missing a center of attention. Crucial eye candy, if you will."

I stared at him. "What the hell are you rambling about?"

He pointed at Colt. "My little bro doesn't take his eyes off his pretty jewel, Jade, all night. Even when she disappears down the hall to the storeroom, he stares all dreamy eyed that direction just waiting for his pretty little vision to return."

Colt leaned back. "You're fucking nuts, do you know that?"

Slade waved him off. "No, it's all right, bro. She's a damn picture. I don't blame you, and I'd probably do the same if I had someone like her." He turned to me. "And you, my ever-serious big brother, well we all know who you watch. Actually, watch isn't the right word for keeping an eye on someone so fiercely it seems you just might tear the head off of someone who dares to breathe air too close to Street. But that's old news. Now there's me. Mind you, tonight there's been a nice parade of beauties in and out of this place." He lifted up a napkin that had a phone number on it. "Including that sweet redhead who was in town to visit her aunt. But there is never that one girl who the spotlight always follows for me. I'm kind of pissed about that. I feel like I'm missing out on some kind of club membership or something."

Colt poured himself the rest of the beer. It was the last pitcher of the night. Almost everyone had cleared out of Lazy Daze but we were waiting until Jade and Amy were done with their shifts. "Damn, Slade, are you eating those funky mushrooms again, cuz you're talking like you're batshit crazy."

"Nope this is just me reflecting."

"Yeah, the reflecting bullshit again," I said.

Slade looked at me. "You, buddy, need it more than anyone. Not many guys can be completely nuts about a girl and yet, so boldly ignore it as you do."

"Yep, he has a point," Colt chimed in.

"Fuck. Is it closing time yet?" I glanced up at the clock above the bar.

"Hey, we're just looking out for Street," Colt said. "Just in case you're stupid enough to let her walk away."

I pulled my eyes from Amy, proving Slade's earlier point, and raised an angry brow at Colt. "You must have strapped on your steel balls tonight, eh little brother?"

"Sure did. Someone's got to stop you from being your own worst enemy."

I sucked down the rest of the beer in my glass. "Think I'll wait outside. You guys are exceptionally irritating tonight, which says a lot because both of you are like that itch you get on the bottom of your foot when you're wearing a boot. The one that can't be scratched no matter how hard you try to get rid of it."

"You just stomp your foot really hard," Slade suggested, and gave a demonstration with his own foot.

"Stomping the annoying itch—" I nodded. "First smart thing you've said all night." I slipped out of the booth and headed across the bar.

Amy glanced up from her task of stacking clean glasses. "Where are you going?"

"Just need a smoke and a breather from Tweedle dumb and Tweedle dumber, over there."

Her musical and perfect laugh followed me out the door.

With the exception of an unfamiliar, lifted jeep

parked next to the retaining wall at the far corner, the parking lot was down to my bike, Amy's car and Colt's truck. A small red glow, most likely the end of a joint, was making its way around inside the jeep, indicating there were at least four people inside. I hadn't paid that much attention to other customers tonight, but it seemed there had been only a handful of out-of-towners.

I stood next to my bike and pulled out a cigarette. I covered the flame with my hand as I lit the end and took a drag. It was the first one I'd had all day, and it tasted smooth and inviting. It was a hard habit to give up, but I was close. It was only when shit really got to me that I needed to light up. Colt and Slade and their annoying fucking opinions had gotten to me only because I knew there was plenty of truth in what they said.

Jack flipped over the open sign, and I heard the lock on the door spin. I stood by my bike and enjoyed the cigarette while the jeep people enjoyed whatever the hell it was they were smoking. It was unusual to see someone hang around the lot after closing.

Amy's laugh pulled my attention to the door. The four of them walked out.

"Hey, we're going to stop off and get some of that cookie dough that you just scoop and bake so we can munch and watch some movies at our house," Slade said as they walked past. "You coming or do you have other plans?"

I looked over at Amy. "You should come back with us," she said.

"Yeah, all right. But only if these two dorks don't talk to me."

Colt held out his arms. "What? Then you're taking away our entertainment."

"Those are my terms." I walked over to the trash and tossed in my cigarette. Slade, Colt and Jade climbed into Colt's truck. I walked Amy to her car.

She peered up at me. "You don't have to come with us. I mean if you have plans..."

I reached up and tucked a stray strand of her copper hair behind her ear. "No plans. I'll be right behind you." I kissed her forehead and headed back to my bike. From the corner of my eye I saw Colt's truck leave the parking lot. In the distance I heard the jeep fire up. I stopped to pull the keys out of my pocket. Headlights swept around and glanced off the tinted windows of the bar. Tires shrieked behind me.

"Hunter, watch out!" Amy screamed.

I spun around. Amy had jumped back out of her car. The jeep was racing toward me. I caught a glimpse of the driver as I flew out of its path. My shoulder took most of the impact as I dropped and rolled across the pavement. The sound of metal being twisted and broken filled the night air.

"Amy get in the car!" I yelled as I jumped to my feet

in case they circled around. Dust kicked up as their tires skidded over the rough asphalt heading to the exit. Apparently, the sore losers from the poker game were satisfied that they'd gotten their revenge.

I couldn't bring myself to look at my bike. Rage seethed through me and I tore after the jeep. I lunged forward and grabbed the bumper but the driver gunned it. They flew toward the road but screeched to a halt as Colt's truck pulled up to block them.

"Stay in the truck," I heard Colt say to Jade as he and Slade jumped out. Slade had a tire iron in his hand. He was smacking it against his opposite palm. I raced up the passenger's side and yanked open the door before the guy could lock it. It was the guy I'd nailed with my fist until Fletch stopped me.

I reached in, grabbed his shirt and dragged him from the car. Slade was doing a nice number on the jeep with the tire iron, and Colt had the driver face down in the dirt.

The guy in my grasp swung wildly at me, hitting me once on the shoulder.

"Shit, did I do that to your nose, or was it always that fucking crooked?" I pulled my fist back. "Let's see if I can fix it."

He shut his eyes and braced for the pain. I swung my fist into his stomach instead. As he doubled over in agony, an arm reached around and put me in a stranglehold. They'd been keeping their bigger friends in the backseat. I grabbed the guy's arm and heard a switchblade flick open right next to my ear.

"You asshole," Amy's voice came from behind. The guy was thrown off balance as my little wildcat jumped on his back putting *him* in a stranglehold with both her arms. I freed myself. He managed to swipe my shoulder with the blade just as I kicked his knee. He yelled out and stumbled forward. Amy spilled off his back. I caught her before she dropped to the ground.

Jade had moved the truck back into the parking lot. Jack was watching the whole thing, swinging a baseball bat from his hand, just waiting to jump in. Colt and Slade were standing with their arms crossed as they watched the sniveling assholes crawl back into their beat to hell jeep holding bloody noses and mouths.

The jeep limped away without any headlights or taillights.

Amy walked up to me and pressed her fingers against the blood rushing from my shoulder. "Oh my god, I can't believe you're bleeding again."

Jade climbed out of the truck. Everyone stood silently and looked at me.

"Friends of yours?" Slade asked.

"Same assholes who left that gash on my face. I won money from them, and they're still having a hard time accepting it." I hadn't turned around. I didn't need to. I could see in all of their faces that it was bad.

"God, sweetie, I'm so sorry," Amy said quietly.

"We can put it in the back of the truck," Colt suggested.

I turned around and walked back to the bike. It was in a several pieces, mangled well beyond looking like a motorcycle. It was a tweaked heap of chrome, metal and rubber. I bent down and picked up the side view mirror. The glass was shattered. I stared into it, seeing my own reflection in the fragments. I closed my eyes for a long moment. Just like Amy, I'd never had a lot. I had my brothers. I had Amy. And I had my bike.

"Fuck!" I heaved the broken mirror clear across the parking lot. It clinkered into a hundred pieces somewhere in a distant corner of the lot.

Amy walked up to me. She didn't say a word as she wrapped her arms around me. I pulled her against me and held onto her like she was all I had left in the world.

TWENTY

AMY

My mom was humming. It was a completely familiar sound. When I was young, she always hummed show tunes when she was doing dishes or folding laundry. I always thought it was funny that the few times she was cheery enough to hum or sing was when she was performing boring chores. It had something to do with her mind being focused on easy tasks instead of on the bad stuff. Hearing it now, a *Sound of Music* medley, apparently, it sounded weird, misplaced, as if I'd woken up in a different life.

I walked out of my room. Mom was in the hall closet moving stuff around. She heard my footsteps and peeked her face around the open door. The new meds seemed to have finally leveled out, and she was feeling better. Or at least I hoped so. She hadn't done anything too crazy, and she wasn't always sleeping. To me, having her semi-normal was like waking up to a pony on Christmas. If she stayed steady like this, I'd be thrilled and relieved. The occasional humming of show tunes would just be the icing on top.

"Morning, sweetheart."

"What are you doing, Mom?"

"Just thought I'd spend some time rearranging the closet."

"Great." I moved to walk past her.

"Oh my gosh," she said as she pulled a dress out of the closet. It was the lavender dress she'd sewn for my eighth grade promotion. "Do you remember this?"

"Of course I do. I loved that dress."

She held it up against me. "Guess it's a little out of style and a bit too short now." She lowered it and smoothed her fingers over the silky purple fabric. "Your dad was so mad at me because I spent so much on the material. He just never saw the beauty in things."

"No, he didn't." We were having a regular, lucid conversation. These moments had been so scarce lately that I felt like I was standing on a floor made of tissue paper and I'd fall through it soon and land back in crazyville. The sad thing was— these moments, fleeting and rare as they were, almost made it harder when she returned to her other self. They reminded me of the mom who I'd once known and loved to spend time with.

I had hope for the medicine, but I also knew it was always a wild roller coaster ride with my mom. I never knew what was waiting around the next turn of track.

"I'm going to make some coffee," I said.

"Already made."

I looked at her and raised a questioning brow.

"Don't worry, it's perfectly safe. No snail poison, I promise."

"Good to hear." I stepped into the kitchen. My gaze drifted to the window just in time to see Hunter heading down the street. He walked everywhere now, refusing rides from anyone. He looked sad and lonely like a little boy who had lost his dog. He loved that motorcycle and losing it had crushed him. I had no way to make that better for him, and I hated that. He was on his way down to the *Ranger*. He still hadn't found work but spending time fixing the boat seemed to make him feel better.

Mom came in behind me. She caught me watching Hunter. Even with everything she was going through, she knew how strong my feelings were for Hunter. When I was a teenager, Mom and I had gotten into more than one all out scream-fest about him. She constantly prefaced her side with how badly she felt for the boys and she'd do her little tongue clicking thing but nothing else that would actually help them. Then she'd remind me that I was ruining my reputation by hanging out with them. My retort had always been that my reputation remained solidly crappy with or without the help of the Stone brothers. But as we grew older and as my mom's mental health deteriorated, she'd given up on the fight. Her arguments, she knew, had never made a bit of difference. The Stone brothers were always going to be a part of my life.

"Where's Hunter off to so early? He looks tired. Those boys. That father sure left behind a mess." She was extraordinarily normal this morning, and it was slightly scary. The words 'the calm before the storm' kept floating through my head.

"They're doing fine, Mom. You don't have to worry." I pulled my eyes from the window as Hunter turned the corner out of view. My mom even looked more mom-like today with pink cheeks and her hair neatly brushed into a ponytail. "Hunter had some spare time, so he's fixing the engine on the *Ranger*."

Her eyes rounded. "The *Ranger*? Your dad's boat? Why on earth is he doing that?"

"The boat is just sitting there decaying from salt and sun. I'm sure we could still get some good money for it."

She shook her head and reached for a cup. "What would your father say?"

I looked at her. "Nothing. He's dead, Mom. Remember?"

Confusion crossed her face for a second, and I

thought the moment of clarity was gone. But then she smiled. "Of course, I know that." Her tone wasn't completely convincing. "I just meant that boat was his pride and joy. He would be distraught to know that it was being sold."

"Uh, excuse me for pointing this out, but shouldn't we have been his pride and joy instead of that rust-eaten trawler? We need the money, Mom."

She poured some coffee and took three big spoons of sugar, a recent habit she'd started of turning her coffee into something that resembled syrup. "That's fine, sweetheart. Whatever you think is best."

"It's only in the fixing stage right now anyhow, so you don't need to worry about it." I sipped some coffee and watched as she pulled out the kitchen chair and sat with her sugary drink. "Mom, those new pills really seem to be helping you."

She lifted her eyes to me. They were my eyes only more glazed and slightly less focused. "What pills, Amy?"

"The new ones that Dr. Peterson prescribed."

She waved her hand. "Oh those. I stopped taking those two days ago. They were making me terribly sleepy."

I put down my coffee and crouched down next to her. "Do you mean you haven't been taking the pills from the weekly pillbox that I set up for you?"

"Nope, and I feel just fine."

"Mom, you can't just stop like that."

"I'm fine. I was thinking about making some spaghetti tonight. What do you think?"

I straightened and stared down at her. "We'll have to go see the doctor then, Mom. He'll find you something else to take."

"For what? I don't understand, dear, why you're so upset. I'm perfectly fine." She smiled and sipped her sweet coffee.

"Oh, Mom, if only it was fine. If only we could just capture these last few minutes and keep repeating them over and over again. But we can't." I kissed her forehead and headed out to work on the yard and wait for that damn storm.

TWENTY-ONE
HUNTER

"Ferncreek Road? You're taking me to the old Kingston place. Why the hell are we going to visit that ancient ruin?" I asked.

Colt grinned. "You'll see. While you've been moping around the house, crying about all your bad luck, your little brother has been planning and hustling and thinking."

"I know that's supposed to sound promising but it's doesn't. Hey, Rincon left me a message to call him today. I hear he wants us to come back. He couldn't find anyone else to work his water route."

"Not interested," Colt said sharply.

"Really, cuz I was sort of thinking that I'd like to be able to at least eat this next month. Especially because I don't have too much else going on in my life. At least I can shovel burritos and pizza in my face and give myself a fucking heart attack."

"Don't give me that bullshit. You've got a chunk of change saved up just like me, and it's time to start putting that money to work. What did the insurance company say about the bike?"

A disgusted laugh spurted from my mouth. "Can't get enough to replace the damn tires let alone the bike. But I already figured that. I wasn't paying enough premium to get it replaced. I figured if I totaled the thing, I'd be dead too so it wouldn't matter. Never expected some jackasses to run it down with their car."

"What about those guys?"

"It's done. I broke the guy's face and took plenty of their money. I told Fletch I'd be avoiding his poker games from now on."

He turned up the long driveway to the property. The Kingston place was a decaying fossil of a house. Admittedly, it had character and looked like an old Victorian home you'd see in a gothic horror flick, but it had been boarded up for so long it was a wonder that it hadn't just turned to dust and disappeared. The Kingston family had owned a successful fleet of fishing boats and they'd had big money back when our dad was a kid. But health problems, divorce and one of the sons landing in jail for murder had destroyed the family fortune. The place had landed in the care of a distant cousin. But he had no money or time to keep the place up. For awhile he'd tried to sell it at an extra high price, but the economy in the area had been bad and there had been no takers.

"Don't tell me you're thinking of buying this shit hole to fix up."

Colt nodded. "Actually, I'm thinking that both of us, and Slade if he's interested, should buy this shit hole. We could fix it up and sell it."

"You've lost your fucking mind."

"Probably." He parked the car and we got out.

Weeds had choked off the brick path leading to the front doors. Colt tramped over them and I followed.

"I'm half expecting some ghost to float out of one of those dormer windows," I said.

"I think that just adds to the character of the place."

"Yeah, it also makes it a realtor's nightmare."

He swept his arm around. "Million dollar view, buddy. We fix this place up to its former glory, and it could turn a solid profit. I've already talked to the cousin who owns it. He's ready to do a cash deal to avoid realtor fees and shit."

"It'll cost a fortune to fix."

"Probably, but we could do a lot of the work ourselves. What do you say, bro? Now that I'm with Jade, I need to turn myself around. And you and Amy —" he stopped. "Anyhow, I think this could be good. I'm done with going out on the water never knowing if we're going to come back. I don't want to do jail time either. I've got someone I need to take care of now. I'm done trying to trash my life by doing illegal shit. Even our asshole dad worked for a living."

I looked his direction. "Have you been talking to Amy or something? She was handing me that same line."

"Because it's true."

I looked at the house. Wood was rotted, glass was broken and the facade seemed to be screaming for a merciful death. I glanced at Colt. He was excited about this. For more than two years, I'd been dragging him out on drug runs. I'd been in charge of my brothers since I was eighteen. I was thrown unwillingly into the role of father when I'd never had a model of what a good dad should look like. The only thing I had learned was that everything my dad had done, his beatings, his iron fist control, was wrong. So I'd done the opposite. My brothers and me had basically run fucking wild doing whatever the hell we liked. We'd been freed from a horrible prison once the old man had kicked. The chains had come off, and we could do whatever we wanted. Only the lines between right and wrong had always been blurred. So many times, our dad had tried to beat what he'd called 'sense' into us, but he never told us what that 'sense' was.

I took hold of the porch railing and gave it a shake. It wobbled. "Feels like the whole house might come down with it." I glanced back at Colt. "It's going to take a lot of fucking work."

"Yep. I'm looking forward to it."

I took a deep breath. "I'm in."

TWENTY-TWO

AMY

Things had been smooth as cream for a day. My mom had busied herself cleaning every drawer and closet in the house, and she'd gone through her entire catalog of show tunes. But, by evening, right as I was getting ready for work, the humming, closet cleaner was starting to see small green bugs on the kitchen wall. I'd had no choice but to go to work. A cancelled shift was too much of a money loss. I made her a grilled cheese and then tucked her into her bed to watch television. She was dozing soundly by the time I picked up my keys to leave.

Thankfully, she was still fast asleep when I got home. I plopped down in my dad's chair and turned on the television. My phone buzzed. It was Hunter.

"Hey, I'm here with the Bozo twins playing video

games and eating pizza. I heard your buzzing little car pull in. Why don't you come over?"

In his head, he'd squared away everything between us by ignoring all the stuff I'd brought up. As far as he was concerned, everything should just stay as it was. Hunter was good at ignoring anything that might take too much time or emotion or thinking. Because he'd lost his motorcycle, I'd dropped the subject for now. My own selfish need to be part of his life in some way had helped me to drop it. But deep down, the constant ache was still there, chipping away at my heart and soul.

"I need to hang out here. My mom sort of decided to just drop her meds cold turkey, and I'm waiting for all the damn shoes to drop. I'm kind of tired anyhow. But save me some cold pizza for tomorrow."

"Yeah, right. Slade's here, so I'm pretty sure there won't be anything but a few crusts left." He paused. "Hey, Street, if you need me just call. I'm only about thirty steps away."

I couldn't figure out exactly why his last words impacted me so much, but my throat clamped up and I could barely say the word bye. I hung up and glanced out the window toward their house. The light from their television flickered through the thin curtains on their front window. I leaned back in the easy chair and rested my head. It had always been a comfort having the Stone brothers so close. I never felt alone or unsafe with them just a few yards away.

Light footsteps padded down the hallway and my mom emerged. She once again had the flamingo beach towel wrapped around her bathrobe. Her face was down, and she was muttering about something. They were back. Her inner demons, the voices that plagued her night and day, were back.

"Mom, do you want me to make you something to eat?"

She ignored me and continued on her mission, whatever the hell that mission was. She went into the kitchen for a few minutes and cradled something in her hands as she walked back through.

I was bone tired and didn't even lift my head from the chair as she shuffled back through. Then, unexpectedly, she stopped just before disappearing back down the hallway. She turned to me, and the rational, clearheaded expression from this morning flashed across her face. "Whatever you do, sweetheart, my beautiful Amy, chase happiness no matter how long it takes." Then her shoulders rolled forward. She shut the towel tighter around herself and whatever snack she'd grabbed from the kitchen, and she plodded back to her room.

I watched the empty doorway wondering if in my groggy state, I'd just imagined those last few seconds.

I rested my head back. My lids felt heavy from the long day. I let sleep take me away from reality.

IT WAS A CRACKLING sound that woke me. As I urged my mind out of the dream I'd been having, I tried to reconcile the sound with anything I'd ever heard before. But I couldn't. A loud snapping sound made me jolt forward. The haze in the room was not in my head. It was smoke. Not a burnt toast or singed popcorn smoke. It was a horrible, acrid smoke as if chemicals and fabrics and things were being consumed by fire.

I jumped up. The darkness in the hallway had been replaced by a thick gray mist. I raced to my mom's door and grabbed the doorknob. It was hot but I wrapped my fingers around it and turned it. The door didn't budge. I'd removed the lock long ago, but something was blocking it and keeping it from opening.

"Mom!" I pounded on the door. "Mom, let me in!" I jammed my shoulder against it and pushed with all my weight. Whatever was on the other side weighed more than me. It was as if she had moved all her furniture in front of the door. Smoke curled up from beneath the door like vicious gray fingers, teasing me, letting me know that I had no chance to get in.

I stepped back and ran toward the door. I rammed

the door and sharp pain tore through my shoulder. I kicked the door again. "Mom, go out the window!" I screamed.

A sound behind me made me spin around. It was the drapes in the front room. The flames had crawled up and over the roof. Fire was taking the whole house. Heat and smoke filled the narrow hallway. As I ran for the front door, Dad's old easy chair, the place I had just been sleeping, burst into flames. Fire quickly traveled from the front window drapes to the faded green curtains on the front door.

I raced to the kitchen. The window hadn't been opened in years, and it was glued shut like cement. Panic and shock made me freeze. I had no idea which way to go. The flames were winning, and I couldn't seem to outpace them.

I was struggling to breathe, and my eyes watered from the smoke. I stooped down. I needed to get to my bedroom and out to the yard so I could get to my mom's window. The smoke and heat in the hallway were so bad I had to feel my way along the walls. Paint was blistering off the plaster. I couldn't catch a decent breath. I yanked my shirt up over my mouth and nose, but it did little to filter the air. It felt as if all the oxygen in the house had been replaced by bitter, pungent chemical smells.

Dizziness overwhelmed me, and I dropped to my

knees to crawl. The pain in my shoulder made my right arm weak, and I had to pull myself along with my left. But I could no longer see where I was going. I smacked my head hard on the edge of the bathroom door.

"Mom," I cried weakly. Tears flowed from my eyes. I was suffocating. I curled into a ball and waited for the flames to take me.

TWENTY-THREE

HUNTER

"What the hell are you burning, Slade?" I called from the dark of my room. I shook off the sleep and sat up.

"Holy shit!" Slade yelled. "Amy's house is on fire."

I shot out of bed and pulled on my jeans. I grabbed my shoes on the way out the door and hopped into them as I raced across the front yard. Several of the neighbors had stumbled out of their houses. Mr. Ames, who lived across the street, was on the phone calling the fire department. Flames were already shooting up from the roof, and the whole house was surrounded by smoke. Slade reached the front porch just ahead of me.

My heart was pounding so hard I could feel it in my throat. Slade reached for the doorknob, but his hand flew off. "Fuck! It's too hot."

"Get out of the way," I yelled. Slade moved aside, and I ran at the door and kicked it in. It was half melted by the heat and peeled away from its hinges. Blinding smoke billowed out.

"They're on their way," Mr. Ames called from the front yard. "You boys can't go in there."

I hadn't had time to pull on a shirt, so I covered my nose and mouth with my forearm and forged through the smoke and fire. It was hard to see anything, but I heard Slade's footsteps right behind me. The front room was engulfed in flames. The heat seared my shoulders and arms.

"You with me, Slade?" I called, no longer able to see more than a foot in front of me.

"I'm with you. Fuck, I can't breathe. Where is she?"

"Amy!" I yelled. There was no response. All I could think was— if she was dead then I'd just follow her right into the flames. I wasn't going to make it without her. No way to live without her.

Slade had broken into a coughing fit behind me.

"You all right?" My voice was being choked off by the bitter ashes in my throat.

He put his hand on my shoulder. "I can see the white edge of the hallway door." He turned my shoulder in the right direction, and we pushed through the blistering heat. The entire house was a furnace, and somewhere inside the raging hell was my angel.

"Amy!" I called.

Then, somehow, through the clamor of wood and rafters falling in on each other, I heard a small cry. I waved my arms around to clear the smoke. There, curled up in a corner of the hallway was the girl I loved. "Amy, fucking hell, baby." I couldn't remember the last time I'd cried. I'd learned to turn off tears when I was a kid because they only made my dad swing his belt harder.

I grabbed her up in my arms, and she clung to me.

"Where's your mom?"

She wriggled to free herself from my arms. "My mom, she's still in her room. She blocked the door." Her sobs were strangled by a coughing fit. I handed her off to Slade. "Take her outside now."

"No, man." Slade's voice wavered. "You need to get out too."

"I'll be right out." A large slice of the family room ceiling lost its tenuous grip on the beams. It fell to the floor right next to us. Sparks flicked off of Slade's arms as he held tightly to Amy.

"Get her out of here!" I yelled.

Slade dashed through the ashes and flames and out of the house. I forged a path through the smoke back to the hallway. I reached her mom's bedroom door. It was too hot to touch. I braced myself against the opposite wall, the searing plaster was blistering the skin on my back as I shoved the door with both feet. The heat and smoke and lack of air in my lungs made it take several good pushes. More smoke billowed out from her room. I lowered my face and squeezed inside. I shoved the dresser away from the door. The bed was completely engulfed in flames.

I stumbled back to avoid being caught by them and tripped hard over something. My tailbone smacked the dresser. I swept the smoke from in front of my face, and through the hazy clearing, I saw Amy's mom stretched out on the floor. Her robe was singed and her face was still as death. I jumped up and swept her up into my arms. She felt like a ragdoll, lifeless and filled with cotton. I could hear sirens growing louder. Red spinning lights lit up the curtain of smoke, making it glow red like the surrounding flames.

My chest, throat and eyes burned as if someone was taking a blowtorch to them. I crossed the front room in four big steps. The outside air, even clouded with smoke, felt like cool water rushing over my singed skin. Fire trucks and the flashing lights of police lit up the street making the whole damn scene like a clip from a movie.

The top two steps were glowing with heat. I stepped over them and busted through the shield of ash and smoke that circled the house. Dozens of people had gathered on the sidewalk and street to watch. There was yelling and the firemen were calling orders to each other. A loud cheer went up as I stepped onto the front lawn. I could hear Amy's small cry as it squeaked through the chaos.

My eyes followed the direction of the sound. She was yanking off her oxygen mask. She pushed away the restraining hand of the medic and came racing toward me. Her mom hadn't moved one muscle since I'd picked her up from the floor. When my mom died of an overdose in her bed, I had grabbed her and tried to make her sit up. I was a kid, and in my shock I'd convinced myself that if I sat her up, she'd start breathing again. But as I held her, I knew I was holding death. I looked down at the woman in my arms. I was holding death again.

Amy leaned down over her mom's face and kissed her. "Mom, wake up." She patted her ash covered face. "Mom."

A medic took her from my arms. He was a big guy, maybe thirty and the look he shot me as he took Amy's mom from me assured me he knew what holding death felt like. He carried her to the waiting gurney.

"I was so scared—" she sobbed as she fell into my arms. "Hunter—" her words broke off.

I led her down to the ambulances. Slade was sitting on the back of one getting some burns treated and wearing an oxygen mask.

He looked at me over the mask. I shook my head just slightly, not wanting to let Amy see. She held tightly to my arm but was in too much shock to notice. But Slade saw. He dropped his face and his shoulders sank down.

Mr. Ames walked up to us. We hadn't spoken in a long time. He was one of the neighbors who liked to look the other way when one of us drove up.

He stood in front of me and looked me right in the eye for the first time. He looked pretty shaken. "It's funny, you form an opinion of someone and then something, ignorance, I suppose, makes it stick as if it is written in stone. I'm sorry, boys. I had it all wrong." He stuck out his hand for me to shake. I took it. "We should have done more—" he said with a crack in his voice. "Back when you boys were young—" He turned his face for a second.

I patted his shoulder.

The medic walked up. "We need to look at these burns, Mr. Stone."

Amy patted my arm. "I'm going to watch them work on my mom. I need to be there when she wakes up." A nervous laugh rolled from her mouth. "She'll be convinced the aliens did this, and I don't want her to freak out."

I glanced at the medic with a questioning look. Just as I had done, he shook his head slightly to let me know what I already knew. "I just need a minute," I told him. He nodded.

Amy turned to walk away. I wrapped my arm around her waist and pulled her back against my chest.

"What are you doing, Hunter? I need to be there. She'll be scared to death when she comes to."

I picked her up into my arms and carried her past all the spectators and to Mr. Ames's front yard, away from the chaos. She wriggled in my arms. "What are you doing?" she asked, sounding more frantic. "Hunter?" Tears fell from her eyes. She kicked out and pushed free of my arms. I grabbed her before she ran. Again, I pulled her back against my chest and wrapped my arms around her.

"No," she cried. "No!" She dropped to her knees and I knelt down behind her. "No. You're wrong." She pounded my arm with her fist, but I held her. She crumpled in front of me and I spun her around and pulled her against me.

"She was humming this morning," she sobbed. Her tears ran down my chest as she pushed her face against me. "She was humming show tunes."

I wrapped my arms around her and held her tight.

TWENTY-FOUR

AMY

It was a dreary, foggy day. I'd hoped for a better one for my mom's send-off. She deserved at least that, some sun to warm the breeze as it carried her ashes away. The five of us, the brothers and my best friend, Jade, my only family now, stood along the starboard side of the *Durango* and watched the gray soot scatter over the choppy, emerald green water. The ashes stayed on the surface for just a brief second giving it an almost iridescent sheen before dissolving into the cold, briny water for good. Now she'd be with my dad. It was what she'd wanted. I could still remember the conversation well because, like the morning before her death, she'd had one of those completely rational moments. We were eating some donuts I'd brought home from the store, and she told me that when her time came she wanted to be cremated and her ashes scattered on the sea. She added that she was holding out hope that dad would be a nicer entity in the afterlife.

Jade put her arm around my shoulder, and we pressed our heads together. My throat thickened as I thought about how lucky I was to have my friends. For days I'd been convinced that Mom had killed herself. I blamed myself for not stopping her to see what she'd taken from the kitchen. I assumed it had been our candles and matches for emergencies. She'd had that lucid moment, giving me the advice to chase happiness, and I had pieced it together as a sort of suicide note.

But all my assumptions had been wrong. The fire inspector and the coroner had both concluded that the fire had started in the wall, an electrical wiring problem. Mom had died of asphyxiation. I puzzled it out that the dresser had been in front of her door to keep out aliens. She hadn't planned her death. She'd been a victim of her rampant paranoia. I still hadn't squared away my feelings about it. I wasn't sure which would have been easier to hear— that she'd taken her own life or that she'd died accidentally. Either way, I'd lost her for good.

Colt pulled a bottle of vodka out from under his coat. He held it in front of me and flashed that easy smile of his that suddenly made the day seem less gloomy. "It's that weird marshmallow flavored kind you like."

I took the bottle. "I like it when it has chocolate liqueur and whipped cream. Not too sure about it straight." I twisted off the top. "But today, anything will work." I hopped on my toes and kissed his cheek. "And thank you for thinking of it." We all gazed out at the rippling water. The ashes had disappeared, and the small, intimate funeral at sea had been joined by a group of seagulls. There were days when the horizon looked so far away, it seemed you could travel forever and never reach the end of the world. Today wasn't one of those days. Today there was a solid barrier of slate gray between us and forever.

I held the bottle up. "Here's to humming show tunes, keeping out the aliens and the voices being silenced for good, Mom. I'm sorry life wasn't better for you." I put the bottle to my lips and winced as the burning liquid hit my throat.

I handed the bottle to Jade. She lifted it. "I'm sorry, Mrs. Linton, that I didn't know you better, but you had to be cool because you raised an amazing daughter." She took a drink and handed it off to Slade.

He swallowed hard and stared down at the water. He nodded as if he was telling himself that it was all right to say something. "Hey, Mrs. Linton, I never told anyone about that winter you saw me walking into school with a short sleeved shirt." He smiled weakly. "I was freezing my fourth grade ass off. I guess it was my own pride. I didn't want anyone to know. I told everyone I'd found the coat. No one else knew but you and me. And I never really thanked you. Thank you for the coat." I pushed my fingers against my mouth to stifle a sob as he lifted the bottle and drank.

He handed the bottle to Colt. "I guess we all have our secret stories about Mrs. Linton." I looked over at him and swallowed to ease the lump in my throat.

"I think I was in fifth grade when the teacher sent me to the nurse with a raging fever," Colt continued. "I'd had it when I left the house in the morning, but our mom sent me anyhow. The nurse couldn't reach anyone at home, and Sarah was on my emergency card. She rushed over to the school and took me home to her house, even though our mom was at home. She tucked me under a blanket on the couch and gave me soup." He raised the bottle. "I'm sorry, Sarah, about the bad stuff. You were a good person."

Their stories were adding a layer to my mom that I hadn't even known, and hearing them now made me love her more.

Jade pulled out some tissue and handed me one and kept one for herself. There had been nothing salvageable after the fire. My entire life and the remainder of my small family were gone with one misfire in an electrical wire. I'd gone to stay with Jade and Colt. Jade had been thrilled to be able to return the favor of lending me some clothes just like I'd done for her when the guys had found her on their boat.

Hunter had his hands shoved in his coat pockets. As usual, at times when emotions were high, he curled in on himself like an armadillo rounding into his protective shell. I knew it was his way of dealing with stuff, and I was used to it. Growing up, he'd had to be the silent, stoic, 'take it like a man' brother and that skill of being unflappable had never left him. But I knew he'd been grappling with some anger about not getting to my mom in time. Even though she was most likely gone long before he'd pushed into the room, he was still trying to reason how he could have done better.

Colt handed off the bottle to Hunter. Bucking tradition, something that was, ironically enough, tradition for Hunter, he took a drink first. His face scrunched up and he pressed the back of his hand against his mouth as he swallowed. "Fuck, that's awful." He pulled a chrome flask out of his pocket and unscrewed the top. He held it up. "To Sarah. I know I was the last person you wanted to see hanging around your daughter, but you never said an unkind word to me in a world where I was used to hearing a lot of unkind words." He paused. Seeing sadness wash over his handsome face made my own tears flow faster. Jade took hold of my hand. "I'm sorry I didn't get to you in time. And, Sarah, thank you. Thank you for letting Amy be part of my life"—he looked at

Colt and Slade—"our life. We'll take good care of her." His chest rose with a deep breath. "I'll take good care of her. I promise." The silver flask glinted in the few strips of sun pushing through the unstable layer of clouds as he pressed it to his mouth and tipped it back.

We stood there for a few minutes longer, but the steel gray horizon urged us to head back into the harbor. Jade and I stayed at the bow watching the storm roll in while the brothers got the *Durango* back to the dock. Then we all piled into Colt's truck and headed back to his beach cottage.

EVERYTHING in my life had changed dramatically, but nothing had changed between Hunter and me. I was still just as unsure of where I stood with him, and I was still ridiculously in love with the man.

As we climbed out of the truck, the sky grew even thicker with rain clouds. The first lightning bolts lit the sky over the water and the taste of electricity filled the air. I held shut the coat I'd bought myself and followed blindly behind Colt, Slade and Jade as they headed for the house.

Hunter's hand grabbed mine before my foot landed on the first step. "Stay out here with me a few minutes, Street."

I looked back at him. "It's going to rain."

His grasp on my hand tightened. "I know." He led me back to the truck and opened the bed. He grabbed my waist and lifted me up to sit on it and then jumped up next to me. We both pulled our collars up to block our ears from the cold wind.

He gazed out at the ocean view for a second. Then his long lashes dropped and he stared, seemingly, at his booted feet as they hung off the tailgate. "You need to pack up your stuff tonight and come home with me."

"Why?"

"Because your place is with me."

A dry laugh shot from my mouth. "My place? And should I bake cookies for you when you have one of your infamous slumber parties?"

He shook his head. "Told you it's always been you, Street. I don't want anyone else."

"Shit, if only I could believe you. The insurance company will be sending a check soon, and I'll have money to buy my own place. I've decided not to rebuild on the lot. It'll bring back too much pain." I hopped off the truck and walked toward the house. I hadn't heard him follow.

He grabbed my wrist and spun me toward him. His eyes were dark with emotion as he took hold of both my arms and kissed me. My hands were flat against his chest, and I fought the urge to throw my arms around his neck and hold him closer.

He lifted his face. "Marry me."

A laughed again. "This isn't funny, Hunter. I just lost my mom, and I'm about as vulnerable as a sugar sculpture in a heavy rainstorm."

He kissed me again. It was a hard, urgent kiss. Not the kind that led to amazing sex but the kind that told me he was serious. His chest lifted and fell as he seemed to be searching for the right thing to say. "That night when I raced into the house, I remember thinking that if you"—he swallowed hard—"if you were dead then I knew I wouldn't walk back out of that house."

"What are you saying?"

"If you're not part of my life then I don't need to be here. There's no fucking reason to get up or to breathe or to live without you, Street." He held one of my hands and dropped to one knee.

I covered a shocked gasp with my free hand.

"I don't need anyone in this whole fucking world but you. There's no one who knows me like you do. We've been connected forever. It just took my hard skull to finally crack open and realize that I can't be without you. Amy, will you marry me?"

I blinked down at him, speechless, breathless and stunned. "You're serious?"

"I am."

"Then"—my voice wavered—"yes, I will marry you."

He jumped to his feet. I threw my arms around his neck. He grabbed my waist and lifted me off the ground. As he spun me around, I heard cheers and whistles coming from the house. Hunter lowered me to the ground.

Slade was the first to come down the steps. "Was that what it just fucking looked like?"

I nodded and hugged him.

Jade came out next, and I ran to her. We hopped around screaming with laughter.

Colt and Slade each gave their brother a hug.

"Well, damn," Colt said. "My big brother has finally been toppled like a great fucking tree in the forest. But I guess I always knew that there was only one girl who could do the job." He wrapped his arm around my shoulder and pulled me against him. "My favorite annoying pest is going to be a sister now." He gave me a noogie. "I love ya, Street. I'm glad the blockhead finally came to his senses."

I walked back into Hunter's arms and smiled up at him. "Yep, and it's about damn time."

TWENTY-FIVE
HUNTER

I pulled at my tie for the hundredth time. Slade laughed. "You can keep pulling at that necktie, bro, but it's not the knot that's making it hard to breathe." He patted me on the shoulder. "I'm really happy for you, buddy. I know she's been the center of your world since forever and well, you know how Colt and I feel about her."

Colt turned back at the sound of his name. Of the three of us, he was the only one who looked semi-at-ease in a suit and tie. In fact, being Colt, he looked like he could have just walked out of a fucking fashion shoot.

"Little bro," Slade called, "you look like the top of a fucking wedding cake, you know that?"

Colt made a show of brushing off his lapels. "I look pretty slick, I'm aware of that. I'm thinking of finding some career where I have to wear a three piece suit and tie every day."

I laughed. "The only suit wearing career you'd qualify for is being a corpse. Otherwise, stick to fixing up houses. Especially since I sank most of my savings into your newest venture."

The side door opened, and the justice of the peace walked out. Her hair was piled up high in one of those old-fashioned beehive dos, and she had on a dress that looked about as vintage as her hairstyle. She smiled. "The bride is right behind me."

We'd decided not to wait. Amy didn't want a big wedding, and the only people we truly cared about were standing right there with us.

The woman reached her podium and turned on some recorded music. Led Zeppelin's Hey, Hey What Can I Do blared out of the small speaker. It was our song, the song about the street corner girl. My brothers took the time to fist bump each other for adding that touch.

The same side door opened. Jade came out wearing a slim cut, blue dress that stopped just above her knees and had thin straps that were glittering with pearls. She was holding a bouquet of yellow flowers. Colt's shoulders lifted and fell as if he'd drawn in a long, slow breath.

"Easy, buddy," Slade said to Colt under his breath.

Jade walked up to the podium. She whispered something to Slade.

"Really?" Slade asked. "Cool." He hurried down the aisle and knocked on the door.

Amy stepped out and took hold of his arm. It was my turn to have the breath catch deep in my chest. My throat tightened as she walked toward us. Her white, silky dress had the same pearl covered straps. The dress had a tight white bodice and it came to just above the knees. She'd pulled her copper hair into a twist in the back. She was head to toe angel.

Slade beamed as he led her up to the podium.

Amy turned and faced me. Her eyes were glossy with tears, and she was smiling. I reached forward and took her hand. It was shaking a little. Or that could have been mine.

"I'm glad I didn't stop chasing happiness," she said softly.

"I had my happy ending living just fifty yards away my entire life."

It was a quick, simple ceremony. Just the way we wanted it. Colt, Slade and Jade cheered and clapped as we kissed.

Amy reached up with her pinky and wiped her lipstick off my mouth. "I got you a wedding present."

I wrapped my arms around her and pulled her hard

against me. "Damn right but shouldn't we wait until we're in our hotel room?"

She laughed. "O.K., I got you *two* wedding presents. But one of them is outside."

I glanced over at our three wedding guests. "Why do you all look like the cat who swallowed the goldfish? What the hell is going on?"

Amy took hold of my arm. "This way, Mr. Stone." We walked toward the exit and our small entourage followed. We got to the door. "Wait," Amy said. She handed Jade her flowers and stepped behind me. Her small hands reached up to cover my eyes. "O.K. let's go."

"Uh, I can't see because your cute little hands are in front of my eyes. By the way, you're giving me some really creative ideas for that second gift in the honeymoon suite."

"Yep," Slade said, "from what I hear the best sex you'll ever have is on your wedding night."

"Shit, Hunter, you better make it a good one. It's all downhill from here," Colt said.

"Are you two done with the king of stupidity contest?" Amy asked. "Someone open the door so he doesn't run into it."

Fresh air blew against my face as someone yanked the door open. Amy held my eyes, and I took a blind step forward. "Now you can look." She dropped her hands. A Harley Dyna Super Glide was sitting in the driveway of the wedding chapel.

"What the—"

Amy wrapped her hands around my arm. "I sold the *Ranger*. Do you like it?"

"God, baby, I can't believe it." I pulled her into my arms and kissed her.

Slade clapped his hands. He walked forward and handed me the keys. "I say we go back to Colt's for food. I'm starved, and our boy here will need plenty of energy for tonight's activities."

Amy's fingers wrapped around the lapel of my suit. "Are you going to give your wife a ride?"

"Fuck yeah, I am." She squealed with laughter as I swept her up into my arms and carried her to the bike. I climbed on. She yanked her silky white dress up above her thighs and climbed on behind me. She wrapped her arms around my waist and propped her chin on my shoulder.

I fired up the motor. "Hold on real tight, little wife."

"Hunter Stone, I've been holding on real tight forever."

WITH POLISHED WOOD and gold leaf details, the inside of the hotel elevator was nicer than any house I'd ever been in. Colt, Slade and Jade had pitched in and reserved us two nights in a honeymoon suite at a fancy, upscale hotel a couple hours from home. Considering we'd had no real place to be alone— ever— it was like the best damn wedding present in the world.

The elevator door shut, and I dropped our one small duffle on the floor. We didn't pack much because we decided from the start we'd been spending the full two days naked in bed. And I, for one, was anxious to get started on that decision.

I hit the button for our floor and turned around. Amy was standing against the shiny wood wall of the elevator. She was still wearing her satiny white dress, only it was covered by her coat. I pressed my hands against the wall on each side of her and gazed down. "I'm just going to warn you that I'm feeling extremely powerful and possessive right now. And I'm so fucking horny, I'm feeling slightly unhinged. So, when we get into that room, unless you want that pretty dress ripped to shreds, you'd better take it off the second we walk in the door."

She flashed me that mischievous lip curl I knew too well, a smile I had the privilege of seeing every day now. "Why wait for the room?" she said in a seductive whisper as she rubbed her hand over my fly and my rock hard cock.

A low groan rolled from my throat. "That, baby, is

why I fucking love you. Any other girl would have been cowering and holding onto her dress, but you, my erotic little angel, know how to meet my dirty thoughts head on."

She placed her hand on my face. "Say it again. Say, I fucking love you again."

"Amy 'Street' Stone, I fucking love you." I took my hands off the wall and grabbed her to me. My mouth slammed down over hers just as the annoying bell on the elevator rang. I pulled my mouth away just as the doors slid open. An older couple glanced in at us and suddenly decided to take another elevator. The door slid shut.

"Thought they'd never leave," I muttered as I turned back around and grabbed her against me again. The bell sounded again, and I groaned in disappointment.

"No, it's our floor," Amy said.

"Thank god." I grabbed up the duffle and threw it over my shoulder and then swept my extremely hot bride into my arms. She held tightly to my neck as I carried her to the room. She pushed the card into the slot and the door opened. I carried her inside and lowered her feet to the ground.

It was a plush, expensively decorated room. Amy stood in the center of the vast floor and spun around. "So this is what it feels like to be a princess."

"To hell with the princess," I said. "I want my sex goddess. Now what did I warn you about that dress?"

Amy put her finger to her mouth as if she was thinking about it. She smiled at me as she slipped off her shoes. "You know, I only plan on wearing the thing once, and it was cheap."

I lumbered toward her and took hold of the tiny strap. "I gave you fair warning."

"Yes, you did." She laughed as I snapped the strap, causing all the tiny beads to fall to the carpeted floor. I tore the other strap and the dress slipped to the floor and pooled around her feet.

I looked down at the puddle of white silk. "Huh, that wasn't as satisfying as I'd hoped. I was picturing much more ripping and shredding." I reached for her panties and broke the thin band of lace. She looked down as they fell to the floor.

"Actually, those I sort of wanted to wear again."

"Oops," I said as my mouth came down over hers. I lifted her, carried her to the bed and lowered her down against the mountain of satiny pillows. She leaned back luxuriously, stretching like a cat and I watched her as I yanked off my rented suit in record fucking time.

I lowered myself over her and kissed her as I settled myself between her legs. I reached down between her thighs and pushed my fingers through the folds. "God, baby, you're so wet already."

She pressed her hand against my face. "Always. I'm always ready for you, Hunter."

I rubbed my thumb along her bottom lip. "The only thing hotter than this mouth—" I watched her face as I slid my cock into her. "Is the way you look when my cock enters you." Her hot pussy tightened around me. "You're a perfect fit, baby. You've always been a perfect fit."

I moved against her slowly at first, feeling her small body beneath me warm with a flush. She was already close. I knew everything about her. And I loved everything about her. I slid my hand under her ass and pushed her pussy higher. She held tightly to my arms as we both came together. I stayed inside of her, right where I belonged.

I leaned forward and kissed her lips. "You realize that was just the warm-up."

"I should hope so."

I gazed down at her. "Well, Street, looks like it's you and me against the world now. Are you happy?"

"What the hell do you think?" Tears filled her eyes as she pulled my face closer for a kiss.

STONE DEEP

STONE BROTHERS BOOK 3

ABOUT THE AUTHOR

With a long list of amazing romances, *NYT* and *USA TODAY* Bestselling author Tess Oliver has the perfect read for you! Visit TessOliver.com to see all available titles.

Anna Hart is a pseudonym of Tess Oliver and her books include the steamy Stone Brothers and Silk Stocking Inn series.

Printed in Great Britain
by Amazon